A SHARP CR

# TAKEN BY
# SURPRISE

## Diane M. McPhee

**BLUE FORGE PRESS**
Port Orchard, Washington

Blue Forge Press is the print division of the volunteer-run, federal 501(c)3 nonprofit company, Blue Legacy, founded in 1989 and dedicated to bringing light to the shadows and voice to the silence. We strive to empower storytellers across all walks of life with our four divisions: Blue Forge Press, Blue Forge Films, Blue Forge Gaming, and Blue Forge Records. Find out more at: www.MyBlueLegacy.org

Blue Forge Press
7419 Ebbert Drive Southeast
Port Orchard, Washington 98367
blueforgepress@gmail.com
360-550-2071 ph.txt

*For my children and grandchildren*
*with love...*

# ACKNOWLEDGMENTS

When I was in my earlies twenties, I lived in Boston's Back Bay and experienced an arson fire a couple doors down the block from my apartment. A person who died in the fire was familiar to me. Maurice was a cross dresser who I often saw waving and throwing kisses while walking seductively down the street. I was always amused by his outrageous clothes and startling makeup and was saddened by his death. Later, I heard it was a murder. I have kept this memory with me over the years, but it wasn't until my dear friend Susan said to me, "You know that story about the murder in Boston you told me? Why don't you write a book about that?"

Writing a book has never been on my bucket list, but once I got started with the idea, I couldn't stop. My brother Brad gave me a year of online Master Classes and I listened to many authors speak about the process of writing a novel. One advice they all gave was to read. I read three or four books at a time, so I knew I was on the right road.

I want to thank Brad and Susan for giving me the push. I also want to thank Susan for proofreading my manuscript, I still don't get the plurals right. Thank you to my sisters for reading the first draft and telling me it was great! You inspire me with your quilting.

My daughter Beth has been my cheerleader. Every idea I ran past her was given thumbs up... even the terrible ones that I would never use. Thank you, my sweet girl. Thank you to my son Ben who read the book and surprisingly liked it very much. My other two sons promised to read it one day... Danny and Billy... don't forget.

And finally, thank you to my husband, Art. As a lawyer and retired judge, you edited and edited, looking for legal problems. You are so smart, and we ended up laughing at my legal mistakes.

A SHARP CRIME MYSTERY

# TAKEN BY SURPRISE

Diane M. McPhee

# SATURDAY, MAY 14<sup>TH</sup>

S truggling to surface from a dead sleep, even with his eyes still shut, Marko knew he was in trouble. The annoying clang of the antique clock had just shouted out eleven strikes. He was late for something if he could only remember what. His head ached, he could barely force his eyes open, and his mouth tasted like a dirty sock. He turned his six-foot two frame away from the glare of the bedroom window.

Moaning out loud, he wondered what had tempted him to drink so much last night. How did he get home? He vaguely recalled leaving the upscale restaurant with Jerome and getting into an Uber. After that, everything was a blur.

Marko had never been much of a drinker, and last night's outing with Jerome was probably his first mistake. His second was agreeing to try the famous "Signature Martini" at the Boston Ritz Carleton bar, and then follow it with a bottle of Pinot. Unwilling to spend money on the pricey food,

# TAKEN BY SURPRISE

Marko's third and final mistake of the evening had been to order a few appetizers as a substitute dinner. He could barely remember walking out of the bar, or was he stumbling, or being carried out? Marko hated to think of the scene he imagined, 'Just another Black guy unable to hold his liquor.'

Fumbling blindly for his cellphone that was usually on the nightstand, Marko panicked. Where was it? He tore at the sheets and weakly attempted to sit up and balance himself. When his feet hit the floor, he slipped on something that skittered wildly across the room. Marko was relieved to see it was his phone, now half hidden under the computer desk as if for safety. He crawled out of bed to retrieve it and noticed he had a recent voicemail. Steadying his hand, he pushed the play arrow to hear the message.

"Marko, where are you? It's already ten o'clock!"

Damn! He had missed the meeting! He sank back into bed, then sat up so quickly that he had to put his elbows on his knees to stave off the dizziness and surge of nausea that threatened to follow. What a loser he was! Cursing under his breath, Marko felt defeated. He wouldn't phone the caller back. Better to man up and face her in person. She probably wondered why she had trusted him to show up in the first place.

Carla, his boss at the teen center in South Roxbury, was meeting with potential corporate sponsors this morning to urge them to fund their grant proposal for a teen homeless shelter. He was supposed to lead the discussion. Now he'd let her, and the kids, down. Shit! For years, Marko had been working with street kids and knew the desperate need for more services and shelters. Building a non-profit homeless facility would provide more opportunities to those who needed help, and the city of Boston would benefit too.

As a teen, Marko remembered how he had dawdled through the years and tried to stay out of trouble, even though trouble seemed to follow him around. He had been bullied and beat up whenever his brothers weren't around. But he refused to admit who was after him because he feared the retribution for telling would be worse. This was one reason Marko identified with the teens he worked with now. He knew what real fear could do to a kid.

Now, at forty-two, Marko hoped this shelter project might be a pivotal point in his career. Maybe, if he was lucky, the meeting had been successful without him, but a sense of failure filled his spirit.

Reaching again for his phone, Marko noticed the note he had written to himself the night before when he had caught sight of Eddie Pearson's parents having dinner at the Ritz. Their son, Eddie, was an eighteen-year-old addict who was just beginning to trust Marko and rely heavily on the Center's programs. He thought about the hours spent listening to Eddie's excuses of why he was trapped in his addiction, unable to escape the dealers who inhabited his world. Every time Eddie was sent to rehab, he promised to stay off the drugs he craved. But just last week, he was seen speaking with a known drug dealer who had a reputation for serious violence against kids who owed him money. Marko worried Eddie had gotten himself involved in something too dangerous for a teen to handle on his own.

# TAKEN BY SURPRISE

Last night Marko had been shocked to see Eddie's parents lounging casually in the restaurant bar. When he had asked Eddie to set up a meeting with his parents to discuss another possible detox and treatment session for him, Eddie had assured him that his parents were travelling in Europe for the next few weeks. Yet there they were, drinks in hand, very much in town. What a liar that kid was! But then, he reminded himself, all addicts were liars, so why would Eddie be any different.

Marko had only met Eddie's parents one time and knew that Mr. Pearson was a wealthy investment banker, and his wife was an accountant. Eddie often complained about growing up on his own and never seeing his parents because of their time-consuming jobs. Marko wondered if they were aware of how deeply their son was still involved with drugs and how much trouble he might be in. Despite Eddie insisting that he was clean, it was clear to Marko he was still heavily addicted and in denial of the fact that he was in over his head. Like most active addicts, Eddie believed he "could handle it." Nowadays, any sleazy drug dealer might think Eddie's parents were an easy mark and could be pressured to pay big money to get their son out of trouble, especially if he messed up. Marko worried about Eddie and decided to call him before he forgot. But the call went straight to voicemail. He left a message and asked Eddie to call back so they could meet up soon.

Finally stumbling out of bed, Marko reached for his sweatpants and a Nike shirt. He needed coffee. Bare footed, he gingerly sauntered to his updated kitchen and prepped the coffee maker. As the smell of the ground coffee beans wafted from his new Cuisinart appliance, it immediately transported him back to the small two-bedroom tenement house in the back streets of Chicago where he grew up. A coffee pot was always on the stove, and now the strong coffee aroma conjured the image of his parents sitting at the old table in their tiny kitchen and talking each morning over a steaming cup.

Marko hadn't thought of his parents in a long time. Once he moved out of the house after high school, he became fixed on his independence. After a stint in the army, and spending four years getting his college degree, thanks to the G.I. Bill, Marko moved to Boston to find a future in the arts. His bachelor's degree focused on music and creative design, but Marko was disappointed when it only landed him a job at a music store.

That was where he met Jerome. Marko poured himself a cup of coffee and recalled that first meeting with his friend. Jerome had been perusing the bins in the music store shopping for Broadway Show tunes and introduced himself to Marko. He explained his love of musicals and that he was a collector of early releases. Marko liked him immediately and learned over the years that everyone seemed to love Jerome. He hung out with a group of drag queens, and his glowing makeup, and exotic clothes made him impossible to miss, while his effervescent persona made everyone smile. One day Jerome approached Marko at the store and invited him to the Dragonfly Theater, where he held court, to see the drag show he was starring in. Marko was pleased and curious, and from that point on his life took a dramatic turn. It didn't take him long to realize he could use his design degree in a way he never imagined. After the first few shows, Marko began working part time designing dresses for the queens.

Marko's reverie was interrupted when his cellphone rang. He saw from the phone screen that it was an unknown number, and Marko knew he didn't have the patience to deal with problems now. He dropped the phone on the counter and then heard the beep of a voicemail. Shaking his head and letting out a frustrated sigh, Marko gave in and listened to the caller's message. Barely making sense in a spray of words, the voice stammered, "Listen man, I'm in some deep shit," and paused for a moment, then continued, "Damn, damn, damn! I need to get out of Dodge... what am I gonna do—should I— nah, that won't work—"

Marko was worried. Recognizing the frantic voice, he immediately called the number back. "Calm down and tell me what's going on."

"There's this guy that's after me who wants to meet tonight and settle up. I owe him—big time! He says he'll go after my family for the money I owe him if I don't show up." He paused. "Oh God, my father's going to kill me! He's finished bailing me out and sending me to rehab." The desperation in the caller's voice was causing him to think irrationally.

Attempting to calm him, Marko spoke slowly, "Okay, let's think about this. Why would this guy want to meet with you tonight?"

"I don't know! He just said to show up and we'd talk."

"Where are you meeting him?"

"That old building on St. Botolph Street. The one at the end of the block, next to the alley." Everyone knew that a couple of dealers used that building to sell their wares. Marko listened further, "I'm worried about meeting there because this weekend it's empty. I heard they have a gross rat problem, and the exterminators are fumigating."

"What time does this guy want to meet?"

"He said around 11:00."

"Okay, I'll come with you. Let's meet at 10:30 in front of the building."

Marko was familiar with St. Botolph Street, which was located between the Back Bay and the South End sections of Boston. It was a residential neighborhood, and like all neighborhoods, there was an element of contradiction. They had a small but vibrant community of thoughtful, committed citizens who worked together and encouraged dialogue, and they also had their share of drugs and dealers. Teens hung out in a building on the far corner to meet the dealers and then used the corridors to get wasted. Lately, there had been several thefts reported in the surrounding area and the police patrols had been increased.

Mulling over the phone call, Marko thought about calling his friend, Alan, and letting him know about the trouble his teenage client was in. A long-time friend, Alan Sharp was a veteran police detective who was known to get results. More importantly, Marko trusted him and his discretion. Over the years they had worked together with Marko giving Alan a heads-up to impending trouble, and Alan helping Marko pull some of his more "active" addicts away from jail and into rehab. He'd even helped a couple of them get into college on the q.t. They had the same objective, keeping the kids on the straight and narrow and keeping teenage crime to a minimum. Still, Marko decided he would wait and call Alan in the morning. He didn't have all the answers yet and didn't want the police on this case for something he might be able to resolve. One thing Marko decided he could do, was to finally learn who the dealer was and give the name to the police.

In the meantime, the day was getting away from him. He had to shower, get something to eat and then spend the rest of the day organizing the tedious paperwork that had accumulated for the three jobs he managed to hold down.

Later that night, just after 10:30, Marko arrived at St. Botolph Street and thought it was strangely quiet for a Saturday night. Maybe the warm May evening had kept people out longer, enjoying concerts or outdoor activities. As he approached the old building, he wondered if the exterminating company had already done their work that day. After waiting across the alley for twenty minutes, with no sign of anyone, he moved closer to the entrance. He thought he saw movement inside. Reaching for the door, he realized it was unlocked. He pushed it open and poked his head inside. No sign of the teen he was meeting. Maybe what he had seen was one of the tenants who had returned early.

Marko walked inside and looked around. No movement. The hallway was lit by a single bulb. It felt cold and dead to him. "Hello? Anyone here?" He didn't want to startle whoever might be there. He took a few more steps in. A sound behind him barely registered before something hard landed on the back of his head. Pain exploded behind his eyes. He landed hard on his knees then toppled forward. He didn't feel the second or third blow. The last thing he was conscious of was the smell of gasoline.

# SUNDAY, MAY 15<sup>TH</sup>

S inking into the worn-out leather swivel chair that claimed the center of the tiny office in the downtown Boston Precinct, Detective Alan Sharp pulled his bulky weight around to his desk and slapped the police report down. Rubbing his eyes and taking in a deep breath, Alan tried to rein in his growing emotions. How could Marko be dead? Marko was not only one of the best teen counselors he had ever worked with, but he was also a good friend. Needing a few moments of privacy to get his emotions in check, Alan rose and quietly closed the door to his office. After years as a homicide detective, death rarely left him feeling so sad and shaken.

Opening the file, Alan turned first to the pathologist's report. The page was topped with the label "Arson/Suspected Homicide," Alan scanned the sheet:

Victim's name: Markus Miller

Age: 42

Race/Sex: Black/Male.

Ht: 6'2". Wt.: 201 Lbs.

Physique: muscular/well defined

Skipping the two pages of detailed pathology findings laid out in obtuse medical jargon, Alan scanned down the page to the summary conclusions.

Autopsy summary: Well-muscled adult Blk male, exhibiting severe fresh burn charring and scarring over 75% of the body. Victim's skull exhibited two distinct impact fractures in the Parietal region of the skull and one additional smaller impact fracture in the Occipital region. Wound in Occipital region likely occurred as the victim was falling toward the ground. Fractures probably caused by a heavy, curved blunt object such as a pipe. Fractures occurred prior to the victim's immolation. Cause of Death: Blunt Force Trauma — Suspected Homicide—Victim's ID confirmed via dental records.

Questions surged into Alan's mind—What was Marko doing on St Botolph Street at that time of night? The report said the fire had been started near the body and raged throughout the building. Gasoline had been identified as the accelerant used—that could have come from anywhere. The canister holding it was found partially melted on the first floor.

Alan's heart ached as he considered what a tragedy this would be for so many people. Marko Miller was well known and respected throughout the area, with a wide network of community contacts and friends. He was a popular figure and mentor to teens who battled addiction, spending hours helping them get to meetings and treatment. He was also employed designing gowns for his friends in the gay community. Alan often called him the Renaissance Man, an older expression that made Marko laugh. Everyone was going to be shocked and saddened to know he was gone. Whoever started the fire knew that Marko was there. Even if they hadn't killed him, they likely tripped over his body. Letting out a deep sigh, and using more force than necessary, Alan kicked back his chair, stomped to the ancient file cabinet across the room, and yanked out his personal folder on Marko Miller.

When Alan sat back down, he shifted his weight to one side, and noticed a slight ache in his chest. His steady habit of burgers and tacos had finally caused bodily reactions like acid reflux. At 5'11", 240 pounds—most of it dangerously in his belly, Alan had recently been warned by his doctor to start watching his diet. Recalling his many sleepless nights, he angrily contemplated his ongoing insomnia which had been just a struggle of forty-minute naps. He was close to retiring at sixty-four and was annoyed with these obvious challenges of aging. But Alan refused to sink into a rut of regret, depression, or despair like many of his peers he overheard talking. He wasn't ready to slow down yet.

Pushing aside the stacks of file folders and papers littering his desk, Alan worked his way steadily through the file on Marko. Cursing when he realized he didn't have a current address for him, Alan remembered to make a note that the files needed updating. This was another frustrating problem for the entire precinct that had to be remedied.

His chair made a loud squawking sound as he leaned back and rang Lloyd Randell, the pathologist. Randell answered impatiently, "Yes, yes, I'm certain. We have Marko's dental records. I'm wondering, Alan, I've noticed that several Boston Precincts have cases dealing with deaths that appear to be caused by arson—but may be homicides related to drugs. I've had a few cases recently where someone tried to cover-up a homicide by setting the building on fire. I wonder if this might be a connection to Marko's being in that building. We all know the work you two were doing with teen addicts," Randell let out a deep sigh, "I'm just putting in my two cents worth so you can catch the bastard who set this fire and killed your friend."

It was true, everyone in the precinct knew that Alan and Marko had a long-standing working relationship. Over the years, Alan had sought Marko's help with teens in trouble because of his dedication and involvement with the teen center. Marco had called upon Alan frequently for help to salvage teens caught up in the criminal justice system. They both knew that the sudden increase in the availability of street drugs had spread addiction problems in the poor, minority, and working-class communities. And increasingly, these same drugs now infiltrated the well-to-do communities of the city. Rich families were suddenly finding their kids experiencing the same issues they unfairly thought only afflicted the less well off.

Marko and Alan worked diligently to combat the denial and resistance to change that often came from well-heeled families, non-profit organizations and politicians seeking to label it a "poverty problem." They struggled to make sense of the blatant social unawareness and tried to focus on a more accurate understanding of teen addictions and insist that more effective actions be put in place. Just as importantly, they worked together to try to save the kids swept up in the plague of drugs, put them back on the path to productive lives and away from the over-whelmed criminal justice system. And now Marko was no longer a part of the shared progress in the programs they believed in.

As Alan read through the file, he knew he wouldn't find much. Marko was private, almost reserved, and wasn't known to share personal information. Alan had met him years ago in such unusual circumstances that they both had laughed remembering the occasion. As a patrolman, Alan had been assigned to patrol the annual Comic-Con event at the Convention Hall that year and Marko was there. The costumed participants were more bizarre than ever, and Alan felt a little unnerved with the crowd. Looking around at the several zombies, half-clad witches and Star Wars characters, Alan saw a guy dressed in street clothes hanging around a showroom. When Alan approached him, Marko mistook Alan for another dressed up participant and started to laugh.

"Great costume!" Marko pointed at Alan's uniform. "I bet the police are wondering if they should arrest you or salute you."

"I am the police," Alan insisted.

Marko threw back his head and laughed. "Show me your ID then."

Alan took out his ID and his handcuffs. "Am I going to have to make an arrest today?"

Realizing his mistake, Marko stepped aside and

started to walk away. "Wait a minute," Alan asked, "how come you're here without a costume? Are you an agent or something?"

Marko explained that he was supporting his friends who were in the next show. He had never been to one of these gigs before and thought it was impressive. Alan asked if he could join him for the show and their friendship began.

Over the years Alan had learned that Marko Miller, born Markus Miller, had grown up in the slums of Chicago as the sixth child of a domestic worker. His father had done odd jobs around the city to support the growing family. Marko had related his family history in small doses, never wanting to reveal more than was necessary.

Alan tapped his pencil on the report, trying to remember the name of one of Marko's brothers he had met in passing months ago. He knew he was a lawyer and lived in the Boston area. Alan met him by accident when he and Marko were having coffee at an outside café one late afternoon. Frustrated with his fading memory, Alan slowly remembered that particular day when a handsome Black man in an expensive suit had stopped and stared at them. Marko had looked away once the two had made eye contact. But the gentleman walked over and greeted Marko. Alan wondered how this elegant man had known his friend and was shocked to learn they were related. After that meeting, Marko was reluctant to talk about his brother, and Alan never pressed him.

Exasperated, Alan reviewed in his mind how he would be able to locate this brother now. He rang Sarah Johnson, who ran the computer and cyber resources section of the department. Taking a breath to calm his nerves, Alan politely asked her to find a lawyer in the area with the last name Miller, first Sidney, and born in Chicago. Minutes later she called back with the name Sidney Miller, a partner at Crate, Friedman, and Miller law firm. Sagging against his chair, Alan knew he would have to visit Sidney and let him know about Marko.

Alan wrote down the address of the law firm. He would wait until morning to meet with Mr. Miller. By then, he may have more information. He hated this part of his job.

# MONDAY, MAY 16$^{TH}$

Maryanne Collier missed work on Monday morning. Being the head teller at Barclay's International Bank in Boston, she was expected to give friendly and courteous service. But she was still shaken after witnessing the horrific fire on St. Botolph Street, where she lived. She told her manager she needed the day off to try and recover. Maryanne sipped her tea and stared out the window of her little studio apartment, trying to recall the events of late Saturday night.

Around midnight, she had been startled awake by the blaring scream of fire engines and police sirens racing by on the street in front of her apartment. Frightened and anxious to know what was happening, she remembers fumbling for her bedside lamp only to realize the power was off. Using the dim illumination that came from the streetlight just outside her window, she grabbed her cellphone and saw the time. Whatever was happening was very close. Unable to determine the ongoing commotion outside, she remained frozen in her bed, unwilling to move. She listened for footsteps near her first-floor apartment door, hoping she would hear another tenant in the hallway who might be able to help make sense of all the mayhem. But there was only silence, except for the sirens and the sound of her racing heart. Maryanne remembers closing her eyes and trying to remind herself not to panic. She was safe inside her tiny studio apartment.

That was when she heard sharp knocking on the outside door to the building. Maryanne's studio was so close to the sound that it had frightened her and caused her to sink farther down in her bed. But the knocking continued, along with someone screaming. Maryanne reluctantly gathered her courage, threw on a bulky robe and slowly opened the several locks on her door to peer out into the empty hallway. Standing on the step outside her building was a tall frantic woman with a little girl, both in apparent desperation. "Please let us in! Please! My building is on fire!"

Maryanne recalls how she froze and stared until she finally recognized the woman. What was her name? Terry or Trudy or something like that. This lady lived in one of the other buildings on the street, just doors away from Maryanne. Belting her robe securely and cautiously approaching the front door, Maryanne undid the lock. The woman pushed her daughter forward, and begged, "Please take my daughter while I go back to my building!"

Beside her mother was a timid child, crying and clutching a limp doll for comfort. Her blonde curls were knotted from sleep, and she was kicking at the glass front door with her little bunny slippers. She couldn't have been more than three years old. Maryanne felt the odd sensation of things moving too quickly to process, but she opened the door anyway and then watched the child's mother run down the narrow sidewalk.

Experiencing a moment of bravery, Maryanne peered further outside to see the people who were crowding around the street. Taking the little girl's hand, they both stepped tentatively to the pavement. That was when she felt someone bump her shoulder as they rushed past. Looking to see who it was, all she noticed were dark clothes. Maybe they were going for help. Turning back to comfort the child, Maryanne quietly asked her name. With a watery half smile, the little girl responded, "I'm Clara." Gathering Clara in her arms, Maryanne hurried back into her building. She wondered at the complexity of fear this little girl must be feeling.

Maryanne's studio apartment was one small room with an adjoining tiny bathroom. Her double bed crowded the room at night, but during the day it reverted to a sofa when pushed back into place. Along one wall was a bookcase full of used best sellers and a small dresser. That was all the furniture the room could manage. Maryanne looked at the small child who seemed to be trembling, "Come and sit on my bed, Clara, until your mother returns."

Attempting to keep her voice calm, Maryanne spoke almost in a whisper, and began to tell Clara stories about brave characters from ones she remembered as a child. Eventually, the little girl fell into a restless sleep.

Clara's mother returned just as the sun was coming

through the window. She looked exhausted and kept rubbing her hands nervously together. "There was smoke damage to my building from the fumes of the fire. I only had a chance to run back into my place and grab my computer and phone." Pacing the few steps around the room, she suddenly stopped and grew unusually quiet.

She whispered, "The townhouse next to mine was completely destroyed by the fire. One person is missing and may be dead. Do you know Marko Miller?"

Maryanne shook her head. "I've heard his name, but never met him. Why?"

Clara's mother stared at Maryanne. "They think it's him… the one who died in the fire." With that said, she quickly gathered up Clara and raced out the door.

When Maryanne closed the door as the woman— Trudy, she now remembered— and Clara left, she collapsed onto her bed. Someone had died! Her first reaction was to flee or hide! She was afraid that danger was creeping just outside her window. Maryanne lay awake worrying.

She was new to big city life and hadn't quite adapted to it yet. She had grown up in a large family in a small town. Her hometown of Spokane, WA, was semi-rural and small by comparison to Boston. Nights in Spokane were very quiet and peaceful. There was little crime to speak of, and sirens in the night were as rare as diamonds in a coal mine. Although excited by the adventure of living and working in Boston, she knew she had felt slightly on edge since the move, and the daily deluge of loud city life didn't help.

Maryanne considered her circumstances. At twenty-three, she had a hard time accepting the frightening reality that she felt terribly alone. She was a long way from her childhood security and family ties. Being able to cope with the challenges in her life was going to take some serious inner work which Maryanne knew was easier said than done.

Sidney Miller was arriving late to work. He finally decided that exercise was more important than stopping for his usual pastry and coffee each morning, so he had parked his car two miles from his office building and walked the rest of the way. The weather always warmed up in May after a long New England winter and today it might even reach seventy. He should have left his warm jacket in the car.

Strolling through the Boston Public Garden, which was rich with historical sites, Sidney stopped to look at the duckling statues and the beautiful trees overlooking the pond. Tourists were already riding the famous swan boats, with their cameras pointed to capture shots of the peaceful beauty of the park. Continuing through the Garden, he watched teens throwing frisbees and wondered when the last time he did this. Did he ever? Heading north, he saw the golden dome of the State House. His law office was located just steps away through Government Center. When he passed by the Quincy Market, he noticed it was already filling up with customers since it was a popular visitors destination, filled with restaurants and shops. Maybe he would have lunch there today.

Sidney loved this city but knew he had never taken the time to enjoy all it had to offer. He was sixty-three and nearing retirement, which meant he would have more leisure time soon. Being a lawyer was more exhausting than the general public understood. Hours of paperwork and reading, rigid deadlines that demanded long workdays, as well as constantly dealing with difficult clients, tired out even the youngest of lawyers. Recently, Sidney devised a system that he strictly kept. If his work was not completed by ten at night, he would turn off his light or read a novel to relax. Even though he sometimes felt guilty for not keeping up as well with caseloads, Sidney knew that life was too short to care.

As he hurried up the steps to his law office, he smiled at the fact that he would walk the same way back to his car after work. When he arrived on the fifth floor, he was winded but energized. This would be a good start to the week.

Sidney's office resembled a gracious den. Mahogany bookcases filled with leather bound law books graced the far wall and adjacent to it was a large picture window that overlooked a view of the city. In front of the window was Sidney's inlaid antique desk that had neatly piled folders on one end and two Montblanc ballpoint pens on the other. The Persian style rug and soft leather sofa on the back wall were understated and comfortable as if they had lived in the office first. Two leather bound easy chairs were pulled up to the desk, waiting for clients.

Sidney's enthusiasm for the day was interrupted when his secretary announced that a policeman was there to see him. He hoped it was not another problem with one of his clients, although he couldn't imagine who might have been arrested. That was usually when the police needed to talk with him. But when he saw Detective Sharp walk into his office, he recognized him and knew immediately it had to be about Marko. Sidney asked Alan to have a seat.

Alan remembered Marko saying that Sidney was twenty years older and had been named after their mother's favorite actor, Sidney Poitier. Alan could see the resemblance, Sidney's appearance and even his formal demeanor had undoubtable characteristics of the actor. His office, too, had an elegance of formality.

Alan wasn't sure how Sidney would react to the news of his brother's death and so Alan began with the facts, "I'm sorry to have to bring you some tragic news. Your brother, Marko, was killed in a fire early Sunday morning." Alan waited a few moments for this information to be absorbed. Sidney sat without emotion, but the silence was profound. He brought his hands to his mouth, forming a triangle around his chin and stared at Alan.

This was the part that Alan dreaded, when the news of death slowly seeps into a person's consciousness and doubt begins to form. No one is prepared for this shocking and terrible news. People usually struggled to recall the last time they saw the deceased and what was said. Their breathing slowed and their eyes found an object to focus on, usually just to keep themselves grounded. And then they asked a question. Always the same question. Are you certain it's him? Or her? Or them? And the police always had to calmly reassure the person that they were certain.

After a minute, Sidney stood up and looked out the window. Alan took this time to tell Sidney the rest of what he knew about Marko's death. "There is evidence it was arson and circumstances suggest that he was murdered." Again, Alan waited.

Sidney finally turned back and asked, "What would you like me to do, Detective? I haven't spoken to Marko in almost a year and that was only briefly. I have no idea what kind of life he was living or even where he lived, as sad as that is. I will have to call my family and let them know our brother is dead. How will I ever explain this? I don't believe he kept in touch with any of us."

Alan took the opportunity from Sidney's mention of his family, to ask some personal questions. "Can you tell me a little about your family? I can imagine they will be very upset hearing this news."

Sidney held Alan's gaze for over a minute. "What would you like to know?"

Alan looked at his hands, took a deep breath, and continued, "Just an idea of how Marko fit into the family. I'm gathering information for references in the file and realized how little I knew about your brother's personal life."

Sidney sat back down in his leather chair. "I'm not certain where to begin, Detective. Marko is... was... the youngest of four brothers, I'm the oldest and the two girls were born five years after Marko. My parents, now gone, were very good people. They taught us all to appreciate what really matters in life, as opposed to what was just plain nonsense. We were all taught to go to church and follow the rules. The valuable lessons about right and wrong and commitment and self-worth were constant. Our home life had many challenges with six children and two bedrooms and both parents working. The house was an old rowhouse in the South side of the city with hardly a tree in sight. But we had each other and seemed to get along just fine." Leaning back in his chair, Sidney sighed, "We all did well and prospered given the opportunities the country had to offer, along with hard work and some timely scholarships."

Sidney stared down at his desk, paused for a few seconds, gathered himself and continued, "We called Markus 'Marko' because of the mark he made when he was in his early teens. He had crazy ideas and wore outlandish clothes. Marko was devoted to music and dance and MTV. He could sing and dance like Michael Jackson and his brothers and even wore a glove on one hand. I remember one day when he was even trying to glue sequins on his shoes. He loved glitter and glamour and entertainment." Sidney almost smiled. "We all knew he was a dreamer. He grew up with the same moral standards as we all did, but he got away with pushing the limits."

Sidney laced his long fingers together, before continuing. "Learning came easily for Marko. But one year, when he didn't do the classwork, it was in seventh grade, our parents made him repeat the year hoping to settle him down. Marko wasn't bothered, he just took it in stride." Sidney shook his head recalling Marko's antics. "Because of the few choices we were given, all the boys in the family entered the army after High School. The four years we spent defending the country were rewarded with debt free college degrees. It was no surprise when Marko went to design school and lived up to his personal dreams. However, he was naïve and thought that as a Black design student, doors would be open to him. He finally worked retail I guess, and then I heard he got interested in designing clothes for the drag world."

Alan began to explain to Sidney how much Marko had meant to him and to the people he worked with. But to his surprise, Sidney stood up and offered his hand to Alan. "I'm sorry, Detective, but I have a client waiting. Could we continue this conversation later? Please, let me know how the investigation is going." They exchanged business cards. Alan nodded and glanced once more around the room before he left.

As he stopped and waited for the elevator door, he looked appreciatively at the sophisticated law office. Obviously, Sidney was doing very well. At least by outward appearances, he and Sidney were light years apart, even though they were probably close to the same age. Sidney's suit probably cost in the thousands, while Alan wore his typical detective uniform of grey slacks, a white shirt, solid tie, and black overcoat. He could have passed for an undertaker. Their backgrounds were also stunningly different. Alan had been raised in the suburbs of Philadelphia by well-to-do, generous, and loving parents. His father was a popular architect and a leader in the community. He had encouraged his two sons to excel and had the means to send them to the best schools. Alan eventually gained a master's degree in clinical social work, much to the disappointment of his parents. He knew they hoped he would study medicine or at least be a Financial Advisor like his brother. But after being drawn into university politics and listening to the racial tension on the streets, Alan could not resist the call to the police academy.

Over the course of the years, Alan's father had advised his son to stop pushing so hard to fix everything. He even advised him to exercise and lose some weight. Most importantly, his father had emphasized that ultimately it was the people and relationships in his life that mattered, and not the fame and fortune. Alan realized he spent the first half of his life like everyone else, acquiring skills, degrees, careers, reputation, family, money, and he found letting go of these things seemed harder as he aged. Habits, even self-destructive ones, had a familiar comfort, like old friends who annoy you. Anyway, Alan thought, he doubted he could change his personality, or image at this point.

Alan's next stop was the crime scene on St. Botolph Street. Arriving in the Back Bay neighborhood, he noticed almost all the buildings were constructed of brick or brownstone. Built in the late 1800's, they reminded Alan of elegant aging ladies because the Bay windows which protruded from each building front were like warm bosoms offering comfort to the community. The houses of St. Botolph Street, like the matriarchs of generations past, had quietly mastered the art of caring for and keeping the secrets of the residents who lived behind the beautiful facades that greeted passers-by.

The Back-Bay area was known as one of the nation's most architecturally important neighborhoods. Alan was familiar with the stories of how young investors years ago had purchased buildings on this street and spent their parent's money renovating them. Some were now worth over $4,000,000 each. At one point in his career, Alan had been looking for an investment and attended an open house at one of these buildings. Because of his father's love of architecture, Alan admired the custom millwork, ornate mantles, and high ceilings of the rooms. Each floor had kept the original brick work on one wall, which was unheard of in new buildings. This old-world charm had been classically combined with all the modern amenities such as gourmet kitchens with custom cabinetry, stainless appliances, granite counter tops and luxurious bathrooms demanded by the rich today. Alan could only dream about owning a place in this neighborhood.

However, here and there a building had fallen into disrepair and not undergone needed renovation. The address where Marko died was a building such as this. Alan understood from the police report that it was owned by a Real Estate investor in the city who had restructured it into several smaller apartments. The place had deteriorated over the years, and from several reports it was clear that recent tenants tended to be part of the nonconformist crowd. The police records also showed a steady stream of complaints of loud parties, drug abuse and petty thefts. There were even indications of drug trafficking at the address.

Alan stood on the sidewalk and saw that the exterior of the burned building was still intact, but there was obvious damage to the inside. The windows were broken, the doors unhinged, and smoke was still hanging in the air. He took out his camera to shoot photos of the damage. He would print these out and have them at home for reference. What was Marko doing there?

An hour later, Alan was feeling tired and dispirited as he drove to the Roxbury Treatment Center for Teens where Marko had worked part time. Carla Tompkins, the director of the center, was a good friend of Alan's.

Carla was a small, greying woman in her mid-fifties, known for her professional competence and her careful, considerate listening skills. She was also an outspoken leader in the community. Carla was tough, knew her way around the system, and had a reputation for getting things done. A self-assured Black woman, she was invaluable to families who needed support during the rising racial tensions that dominated the city and the country.

The center was in an aging strip mall which boasted an array of the regular small businesses common in the area. Located between a Tanning Salon and a Dollar Store, the center was a non-descript grey-paneled building with few signs out front. Alan saw the usual group of teens hanging around the entrance smoking and hoping to find some help or trying to bounce back from a night of drugging. Alan knew many of them had been thrown out of their homes because of drinking, drugs, sex, or violence and most were on various medications. The number of teens in the system was astonishing and there would never be enough centers like this one to handle all the cases.

Alan introduced Carla to Marko five years ago when she was looking for an outreach-worker who could relate to the kids and the community. Carla always felt a kinship with Marko, saw his potential, and often sent him to get additional training throughout the years. He had become one her finest employees.

Carla greeted Alan and invited him into her office. Like many sparsely funded, non-profit offices, Carla's small space was dominated by a grey metal L-shaped desk that sat in front of a paned window overlooking a parking lot. On her desk was a laptop computer and a basket full of hand stressors that people used to help alleviate stress. There was a bank of bookcases on one wall filled with counseling books and photos of teens she had helped. Carla sat behind her desk and offered Alan a seat in a comfortable chair facing her.

He knew that Marko's death would be a shock for her, just as it had been for him. He decided once again to state the facts. "Did you hear about the building fire on St. Botolph Street Sunday morning?"

"Yes," Carla replied, "It sounded like the building was very damaged."

"I am very sorry to tell you that someone died in the fire. It was Marko."

Alan watched as she took in the news, her face falling and her eyes watering. When she finally let out a long breath, Alan reached out to take her shaky hand. He knew how much Marko had meant to her. The horror of learning he had died in a fire was almost too much for her to bear. There was no compromise for this kind of grief. Carla appeared to be in shock.

Alan could barely hear her when she spoke, "We were

supposed to meet Saturday morning. I was upset when he didn't show up for this meeting and so I refused to call him. Now look what happened." Carla started to cry. "I can't... I can't believe he's dead. What was he doing there at that time of night anyway?"

"I have no idea what he was doing there or who would want him dead, Carla. But finding out is going to be my top priority. I have a favor to ask you, I need some information to verify Marko's address and anything relevant you may have on file."

Carla slowly rose from her seat and walked to the file cabinet. Marko's personnel file was thin, containing only his job application, insurance forms, emergency contacts along with his pay information. Carla handed the file to Alan and offered to make him a copy. He was immensely grateful. Before leaving, he asked Carla if she could think of anyone who would want Marko dead. She shook her head. He stepped forward and hugged her, promising to keep in touch.

Alan sat in his car for several minutes with his heart racing. Should he call his doctor or just admit he's feeling overwhelmingly sad and hurt that his friend was dead. He'd always had a difficult time getting over any emotional upheaval because of his habit of internalizing his feelings so often. He had to be more patient with himself. Alan remembered a defining moment in his career when he had been advised by a superior that his only goal was to be 'totally involved and completely detached' from the people he served. Well, this case was different. It was personal. But he didn't want this difficult reality to get in the way of finding the killer.

Glancing at his watch, Alan realized he probably had enough time to grab a sandwich and rush home to walk his dog. Harry was a golden retriever who was named after the wizard kid popular when his children were growing up. Alan hadn't read the books but enjoyed all the movies and wondered just how wealthy the author was now. He heard she wrote another series about a detective he might be interested in reading whenever he retired.

Harry was now ten years old but still had a lot of energy. He would be happy to see his master. Alan had burnt through two marriages and Harry was all he had left. Policemen had terrible divorce rates for lots of reasons, and Alan had struggled not to be a statistic. He was told at one time that staying married to a police officer was often like swimming upstream with strong currents pushing you apart— crazy schedules, taking off-duty work to make ends meet, hanging out with colleagues, and, of course, overprotectiveness. When his second wife left Harry with him, Alan wondered if the truth was more her fear of Alan suffering from depression than needing a dog companion. He'd learned to live with his past and decided not to deal with regrets and failures today.

When Alan arrived at his aging town house, he was surprised to find the door unlocked. Stepping quietly into the entrance, he noted some filthy shoes in the hall and a loaded backpack casually dropped on the floor. This meant his son had decided to pay a visit.

Sam was twenty-four and still trying to figure out where he fit in. Much to his credit, Sam was also a people person. He had attended alternative schools and spent a year studying abroad in college. He'd finished his B.A. in Art and had started a Master's in Art Research, which he had yet to finish. As far as Alan could understand, Sam spent most of his time "interviewing" people for research and not enough time writing his thesis. Although happy to see his son, Alan knew there was probably something Sam needed.

"Hey, Dad," yelled Sam from the kitchen.

Alan looked at his Subway sandwich and was glad he had bought a foot long today.

"Hi, Sam," Alan greeted as he stood in the doorway. "How ya been? What brings you here? Are you hungry?"

Sam smiled his goofy crooked smile and answered, "Fine. I need to talk. Yes."

Alan put the sandwich on the counter and went to get two cokes from the refrigerator. Conversation was going to be delayed as they both tucked into the shared sandwich. Father and son believed that you eat first and talk later.

Harry sat patiently and waited to see if any food would be offered. The house rule was not to feed him from the table, but everyone had a habit of forgetting this. Before Alan took his last bite, he reached down and gave Harry some meat.

"I need to take Harry for a walk. Care to come with us?" Sam was a better conversationalist when moving around. Hopefully, he would tell his dad what was on his mind because Alan had to get back to work.

"And so, Dad..." Sam began as they walked along a

path well worn by dogs and families. "I need a place to stay for a while. My lease ran out and my roommates are moving anyway. I thought I could stay with you until I found another apartment." He glanced quickly at his father, looking for reassurance.

Before Alan reacted, he realized he had conflicting feelings of this being a good or bad idea, flattering or insulting, smart or stupid. As they walked along, he considered how he cherished his solo life and now felt a little guilt about not wanting to share his conveniences. But then, Sam was an adult he reminded himself, and would have some boundaries in place. At least Alan hoped he would.

"Sure," he decided. "Stay as long as you want. Harry will love having you around, too."

Sam didn't tell his father he was leaving school and in the process of looking for a job. He knew he had selfishly spent the last few years casually traveling around without any real purpose, while his peers launched careers or even started families. He often considered his motives arrogant and pretentious, but now he felt the drive to do something productive, to contribute to the world. Sam knew he didn't want to settle for a mainstream teaching career or any job in public institutions, and he felt a pang of guilt with his smugness. He needed this to change. Hopefully, he wouldn't have to stay long with his father.

Driving back to the office, Alan had time to consider living under the same roof with Sam. Was he afraid his carefully constructed life would fall apart now?

Would his routines be judged or ignored? He often brought work home and made important phone calls at all hours, and this could result in confidentiality issues. Alan needed to consider all of this and make necessary arrangements if this was going to work. He had the extra bedroom, so that was easily decided, but Sam would need to take some responsibility for things.

Should he ask Sam to pay rent? He read somewhere that parents who had adult children move back home often insisted on charging rent. What about meals and chores? Do you set up a daily schedule and meet to discuss how things are going weekly? Monthly? Ever? Sam's mother would not be any help because she had her own worries taking care of her elderly parents. And Alan's older daughter had moved to Seattle with her family and was exhausted with work and the two children. Alan would have to manage things on his own.

At his last check-up Alan confided in his doctor that he was worried about growing old, and lately it had become an obsession. He complained about losing sleep at night, due to reviewing and revising his past, present and future. His doctor prescribed meds for his high blood pressure, and then suggested that maybe it was time to talk to a therapist. To top it off, his dentist said he needed dental work due to grinding his teeth at night. Alan wondered if these symptoms were medical or psychological.

Still ruminating, Alan parked his car in his usual spot at the precinct. He reluctantly decided that seeing someone couldn't hurt, so before he got out, he reached into his wallet and pulled out the phone number of a therapist his doctor had recommended. Once decided, he didn't equivocate. Alan called the number of Dr. Rose Gardner and left his name.

The lieutenant in charge of the office greeted Alan at the door and wanted a breakdown of the fire and if the reports revealed it was an arson and a murder. Alan reported what he knew so far from the medical examiner's report. The ME concluded three things: 1) the body was a male, 2) there had been several blows to the head by a blunt object, and 3) the dental records confirmed the victim's identity was Marko Miller. Alan also reported what he knew from his morning visits with Sidney Miller and Carla, then said he had arranged to meet with the condo manager to get Marko's keys.

His lieutenant frowned, "The press is on my heels, Alan, and I need to keep those bastards happy."

Alan nodded and walked quickly into his office. Before he cleared his messy desk, he sat and considered Marko's movements once again. Why was he on St. Botolph Street? Carla said she didn't have a clue why Marko went there. He finally decided to compare Carla's information with his own and start a police file on the murder. She had noted that Marko worked three days a week and was assigned ten teens to counsel. Each week he usually met them at the center, or at their place of residence to ensure they were clean and attending their meetings or required programs. Carla ran a strict program.

She and Alan had discussed many times how teens in Boston were like most teens around the country. Feeling overwhelmed with external and internal struggles, they were dropping out of school daily. These kids were expected to cope with social and parental forces, work, school pressures, and growth issues all at once. Common problems were usually related to self-esteem and feelings of not fitting in. Add in bullying, depression, and grades, and the toxic stew interfered with eating and sleeping patterns. Teens too often felt judged and criticized by their parents and teachers, making them angry and confused. Defiant behaviors emerged as a result and their emotions intensified. To get a sense of control or independence, teens turned to bad friends, drugs and alcohol.

This is where the teen center helped. Carla and her team of dedicated workers were tasked to open channels of clear communication with the teens they served while building trust and acceptance. Carla appreciated Marko's ability to simply direct teens to focus on a future goal, and then help them succeed to get it. What would they do without him?

Alan found his anxiety increasing as he read through the files Carla had given him. He stared at the papers, and realized his concentration was lacking because of his own emotional upheavals. A wave of sadness over losing Marko kept washing over him, but he tried to push it aside. He would have to grieve after he solved the case. Letting out a long sigh, he hoped speaking with a therapist would help ease his mind.

Dr. Rose Gardner had room on her calendar for one more client. She debated about using that time to write since she had promised herself it would be a priority this year. But when she listened to the voicemail from this client, her interest piqued. He was a detective, and this was unusual.

Most men in that profession denied the need of counseling. Rose decided that she would meet with him for a consultation and then make the decision if this was a good fit.

"Detective Sharp," Rose left a voicemail, "I'm free to meet with you today at 5:00 for a consultation. This will be an informal meeting to decide if we are a good fit."

Alan responded with another voicemail immediately and agreed to meet.

**M**aryanne spent the day in a state of worry. When she was growing up, reading was her escape. She never read mysteries or suspense novels because she wanted to keep a certain balance in her life and avoid any insecurity or angst. She preferred to read classics and literary romance novels so her mind wouldn't wander towards danger of any kind. She now thought her carefully constructed life was falling apart from inattention to things like crime statistics and the possibility of becoming an unsuspecting victim. She felt defenseless and with the ongoing investigation happening on her block, she had the chilling sensation she couldn't trust anyone. Sitting in her little studio, fear and loneliness overwhelmed her.

Distressed and unsettled, Maryanne wished her two sisters lived closer. She made herself a cup of tea and realized that the three-hour time difference on the West Coast meant it would be 4:30pm. One of her sisters was probably trying to get her two little one's home from daycare after finishing her part time job. But the other sister was probably still at her desk. She dialed her phone.

"Lincoln High School, may I help you?"

"Hi, Liz, it's me. How come you answered the school phone? Don't you have a secretary?"

"I'm the last to leave. What's up?"

"I just need to hear a friendly voice. There was an incident in my neighborhood this weekend and it's left me feeling on edge. Someone was killed in a fire… in a building four doors down from where I live."

"Oh my gosh! Please tell me you're okay."

"I'm fine. Just a little upset. The police are interviewing people who live on the street, and the whole thing just makes me nervous."

Maryanne knew she could be honest with this sister. Liz was four years older and was known as the brains of the family. It was no surprise when she graduated with a degree in education and was now one of the youngest principals in the district. Growing up, whatever Maryanne didn't understand in class, Liz would patiently teach her at home. She still relied on Liz to help work things out and depended on her good judgement. Their parents were always too busy to notice when problems came up because raising three girls and five boys was exhausting.

"How can I help?" Liz asked, concerned. "Maybe you'll consider moving back here now. I worry about you being alone in that big city."

Maryanne knew her sister would say this. "I just wanted to hear your voice right now. I've got a good job and a couple of friends, so I'm going to stay here for a while." She loved her siblings, but she wanted her independence now.

# TAKEN BY SURPRISE

After a few minutes of small talk, Maryanne said goodbye and promised to call again soon.

Moving back home would mean defeat. Praise was not heard in her family, not even for adult children. Being one of eight, Maryanne could only hope for a nod of indifference. They were all brought up to accept unwavering obedience to the family rules for fear of disapproval. It was tribal in a way, but other families in the neighborhood had similar rules and restrictions. Her siblings were close, but Maryanne wondered if they also built walls around their own little worlds to make it through to the next stage of sought-after dreams. Or were the walls to hide the pain about how they were raised.

Sidney left work early and returned home from an unusually busy and upsetting day. The devastating news that Marko had died left him more shaken than he realized. He blamed himself for not reaching out to his brother, especially after seeing him that day with Detective Sharp. He had failed his younger brother.

To relieve his anxiety, Sidney decided to open the bottle of Pinot he had been saving. Reaching for a wine glass, he also retrieved the electric wine bottle opener that sat in the cupboard. Pressing the button of the opener he saw it was uncharged, even though it was plugged in. "This damn thing never worked!" His frustration increased as he threw it onto the counter and searched through several drawers until he found the reliable opener he had for years.

After pouring himself a glass of wine, Sidney walked into his living room and sank down into the overstuffed sofa.

He wanted to calm down and enjoy his tenth-floor view of the Charles River. It was always one of his favorite scenes.

The wine tasted crisp and full. He missed having wine with dinner, but he knew he had to quit that habit. It wasn't the wine that was the problem, it was the gin and tonic before dinner that made him wonder if he was an alcoholic. One of the reasons he gave himself to quit drinking was that he drank alone. He suspected this wasn't healthy and so he went cold turkey.

When he was growing up, his parents rarely drank. His father would occasionally drop by the corner bar and have a beer, but otherwise, there wasn't enough left-over money for any extras. Sidney was thirteen when he had his first beer. His friend, who was older, told him he had to drink it to be a real teenager. He still remembered how awful it tasted, like grapefruit juice and vinegar. It was only in the army that he acquired a taste for it.

Sidney wondered if Marko had enjoyed drinking. There was so much he didn't know about his brother. On the other hand, he didn't know if any of his siblings drank. Why didn't they talk to each other? Sidney struggled to recall how many nieces and nephews he had now. When was the last time he had visited any of them? He was single and had money to travel. These thoughts left him feeling downhearted.

Taking another sip of wine, Sidney ruminated about making some changes in his life. He saw himself living in a self-contained world of work, without reaching out for friendship or any sort of relationship at all. Maybe he needed someone to help him sort through all of this.

# TAKEN BY SURPRISE

He had called his siblings earlier about Marko and learned that no one in the family had heard from their brother in years. They were surprised he lived in the same city as Sidney. He let them know there was an ongoing investigation and a possibility that Marko had been murdered. His sisters cried and his brothers offered to help. Sidney said he would keep in touch.

Detective Sharp had informed Sidney there would be no identification necessary because the corpse was so damaged by the fire. But he would let him know when the remains would be released. This thought alone made Sidney long to drink.

He stared at the business card the detective had given him. Besides a memorial, he would have to decide what to do with Marko's possessions. He decided to call the detective and make plans to inspect Marko's apartment. He wanted to have as much information as possible before he made any decisions.

Looking at his watch, Alan realized he had twenty minutes to get to Rose Gardner's office. If he took the Charles River Bridge, he could make it in fifteen. He knew the decision to finally get therapy was a positive move. His lack of sleep and mild depression were due to many things, but now that Marko was dead, he felt despair. Trying to calm himself while driving, Alan noticed the blossoms that had emerged on the trees and the gentle breeze that shook some of the petals off onto the street. He knew it was a cliché, but it almost looked like a snowfall. Maybe one day he might finally use the expensive camera he had purchased years ago and take photos of the seasons. The idea of retirement kept occurring to him daily.

As he turned the corner to approach the bridge, he saw a line of cars in front of him. "Damn!" Alan hit the steering wheel with both hands and swore again. This was the day of the crew race for the Harvard team. Did everyone in Boston have to stop their cars to rubberneck? The bridge was full of onlookers and the traffic seemed to be stopped for blocks. How was he ever going to get to the appointment now?

With only fifteen minutes left, Alan called Rose to reschedule, or at least let her know he would be late. The phone at her office went to voicemail. Looking at his GPS he saw that the only other way around the bridge was to drive through the city, which would take at least twenty more minutes. Turning his car around, Alan took a deep breath and decided to follow another route the GPS suggested. He had nothing to lose but more agitation than usual at this point.

As he drove, he wondered if therapy was even a good idea. Maybe he could work out his problems by signing up at the gym or teaching himself meditation. Why pay all the money to tell someone who you don't even know what a loser you are. As he listened to the negative voice in his head, he noticed that his route had been changed to a totally unfamiliar street. He had to trust something, and so he made the turn and hoped for the best.

Alan was now five minutes late for his appointment. His GPS said he was ten minutes away from his destination, which didn't seem possible to him. But he decided to follow the instructions anyway. The road continued until it exited into some sort of industrial park. Now he knew he was lost. He wondered if he had the correct address in his GPS as it guided him to the back of one of the large warehouses. To his surprise, there in front of him was an industrial bridge that rose over the Charles River. He never knew it even existed!

As he drove over the bridge, his cellphone rang. "Detective Sharp, this is Rose Gardner. I see you called."

"Yes," Alan let out a deep breath, "there was a crew race today and the bridge was blocked. However, I found another bridge and can be at your office in ten minutes."

"I'll see you then."

Alan pulled up to Rose's office and parked in a driveway half hidden from the street. The building looked like a chapel rather than a clinic, painted in a hushed grey and possessing subtle stained-glass windows. The front entrance was adorned with spring flowers in bloom and the lawn was freshly mowed. The illusion of peace seemed to hang in the air as Alan knocked halfheartedly on the door. He was greeted by a small woman in her late fifties who had the smile of a saint. "Ah, Detective Sharp! Please come in, I'm Rose Gardner."

Rose escorted him into a drawing room to the right of the entrance. An atmosphere of warmth was felt immediately with soft music playing in the sound system and comfortable chairs gathered around a fireplace. The room appeared to be blessed with the same peaceful air as the building itself. Rose offered tea or coffee before she sat down. Alan declined as he looked around and finally took a comfortable wingback chair.

"Detective, the first thing I ask my clients is why you have come for counseling, and what are your expectations."

Alan squirmed in his chair and gave this some thought. "I suppose I can blame it on my doctor who recommended I see you. I'm having some sleep problems and my blood pressure is higher than normal." Alan hoped this would be a good enough explanation for needing to talk with her. Rose remained silent and so Alan continued, "But I want to say up front that it's difficult to share my feelings with anyone. I guess it's how I was raised, to keep personal issues private, and not complain." Alan raised his eyebrows and suggested, "Perhaps if you give me some ground rules, it might help."

"All right, sometimes I ask my clients to think about creating a mask that would capture your hopes, fears, and expectations. What would your mask look like?"

Alan stared at Rose and then smiled sheepishly, "I'm not much of an artist, but I guess it would be very sad appearing. Or lonely looking, maybe."

"Why is that?"

"Well, to begin with, I don't feel connected to anyone much these days. I've had two divorces and I'm not very close to either of my kids. At work, I have friends and acquaintances, but no one I go to for advice or hang out with. I think I gave up trying and just concentrated on my job." Alan felt like he was complaining.

"Let me ask you, Alan, did you and your former wives have any marriage counseling?"

"No. And I take the blame for this. They both asked me to go to counseling, but I already felt rejected and certainly a failure." Alan let out a deep breath. He didn't like the way this was going. Why was he offering himself up as a complete loser?

Rose seemed to sense his uncomfortableness. "Let's talk about your job. Do you feel successful?

"I'd like to think so. But a job like mine can be time consuming and stressful. This doesn't always make for close relationships. Or maybe this is the excuse I use." Alan knew this was the excuse he used for everything.

"I'd like to know a little about your job."

"Well, I'm a detective, a senior detective. There are good days and terrible ones. Lately, it's been pretty awful."

"Why is it awful?"

"Well..." Alan braced himself to try and hold back his emotions, "take this week, one of my close contacts, who I work with outside of the precinct, has been murdered. This has devastated me, as you can imagine. It makes me wonder if I should take a back seat on this case, but I know I can't. It's too important to make sure whoever did it is found. I owe that to him."

"I'm so sorry for your loss." Rose sensed his growing distress. "It sounds like you need time to grieve."

"Probably, I know the signs of grief. When my father died a few years ago, I hit every single stage. In fact, sometimes I think I am still stuck in the process."

"Why do you think this?"

Alan paused a moment to think. He was feeling put on the spot and wondered how many questions Rose was going to keep asking him. "One of the stages is anger and sometimes I think I've suppressed mine, pretended it wasn't there. Maybe some of my physical problems are a result, I don't know."

Rose smiled gently; she was understanding Alan's reluctance. "Suppressing pain is not healthy. Feelings will come out, one way or another. That's when you certainly can develop physical problems, get into unhealthy relationships, remain stuck in guilt or regret, or even take out some repressed anger on others. Does that make sense?"

"I suppose so. My doctor's treating me for hypertension, my dentist says I have cracked teeth from grinding, and I find myself struggling to talk honestly with my son, who just showed up to stay with me." Alan felt himself sweating and wondered if it was because the temperature in the room had gone up. He was uncomfortable talking about his personal life and wanting desperately to check his watch.

"Alan, this is your time and I want you to feel comfortable. If you want to continue with therapy, we could focus on any aspect of your life, perhaps one that is hurting you the most."

"Well, okay, but I really don't want to examine my old life since I need to get used to the fact that some of its history I can't change. Maybe talking about my anger would be a good start." Alan was wondering if he was even making any sense. But Rose was easy to talk to, and he was thinking that perhaps meeting with her would help clarify some of his anxiety.

Offering a small smile, Rose chose her words with care, "As we age, people continue to worry about problems of their early years, such as children, money, relationships, and possible problems at work. These parts of the past can cause problems now, such as the encounters between you and your son. Does this make sense to you?"

Looking down and then to the side, Alan admitted, "I guess it does. I just know that living with these feelings of anger, and now that my friend has been killed, I feel I'm sinking into a kind of despair."

"You may feel anger, Alan, but also sadness, hurt, loss, and frustration. These are honest, yet sometimes scary, feelings. I would encourage you to consider taking the time and finding the energy to focus on positive new things. This is a stage in therapy called recovery. And it takes courage to try new ways of looking at life."

Alan took a deep breath and then decided, "Can you take on a new client? I sure could use some direction with this because I obviously can't or haven't been making any progress on my own."

Rose looked pleased. "I do have one time available. How does Thursday at 5:00 work for you?"

"I'll make it work. Thank you."

As Alan drove home, he questioned again if therapy would help him. He wasn't always sad, in fact he felt content at times, and even gratitude quite often. But true feelings of happiness were difficult for him to define. He often wondered why he had moved around so many times over the years. At first it was because of his divorces, but after a while he questioned if he was searching for something. Psychologists would probably say he was searching for lost love, or something like that. The reason he bought the condo he lived in now was only because it was close to his job. That was three years ago, and he had yet to feel it was a place of comfort or filled with any memories.

Alan's memory of his childhood home was always how his mother demanded that every area in the house be spotless. She was constantly cleaning, even though she had a woman come twice a month to help her. Alan hated to bring his friends to the house because his mother would follow them around and make sure they kept their hands off the walls and sat on chairs so they wouldn't mess the beds. He envied his friends who got to decorate their own rooms with posters and throw their clothes around. If he even carried a dish out of the kitchen, his mother had a fit.

When Alan left home, he promised that his environment would always be comfortably messy. He liked to know where things were, so he had a desk and bookcases, of course. But he didn't object to leaving his jackets and clothes around the rooms and dishes in the sink. When it got too messy, he would take care of it. But now with Sam staying with him, he felt he had to apologize for his somewhat boring and cluttered living space. He wondered what Sam's priorities were and how they might compromise. Maybe he should reconsider letting Sam move in.

Sam wanted to surprise his father by making dinner. One of the more useful adventures he had one summer was cooking alongside a chef in upstate New York. Although not an expert, he loved being in the kitchen and experimenting with spices and unusual ingredients. When he looked through the cupboards and refrigerator in his father's kitchen, he was mildly amused to see them sparsely stocked. He made a run to the store and decided to prepare roast chicken with steamed vegetables for a more traditional meal. He even had time to bake some rolls.

The delicious smell of home cooking greeted Alan at the door. He was amazed to see Sam at the stove, with a spoon in his hand stirring what looked like gravy.

"Hi dad," Sam said, "dinner will be ready in about ten minutes. Do you want a glass of wine or a beer?" Alan was not much of a drinker, but a beer sounded great. He opened a bottle and sat down at the kitchen table to enjoy this domestic scene.

"So, when did you learn how to cook?" Alan asked.

"You know the month and a half I took off from school last summer? I had a chance to work with a sous chef and he taught me a lot. My specialty is barbeque ribs and I plan on making that tomorrow, or whenever you want. But I've got to warn you, it's spicey." Sam laughed at the thought, knowing his father didn't consider anything too spicey or too hot. He took the chicken out of the oven along with the rolls that were warming, and Alan whistled at the sight.

"I can't remember the last time I had a roast chicken. You're quite a cook," mused Alan. His own mother had been a wonderful cook. Everything was homemade, including the Sunday sweet rolls. She had learned from her mother, and he supposed this education just traveled through the family DNA. But Alan never mastered cooking and relied heavily on take-out. Maybe with Sam here, he would give up the fast food and begin to pay attention to his diet.

During dinner, Alan asked Sam what his plans were. "I don't want to pressure you, son, but I am wondering what you're thinking. How are your studies going?"

Sam considered this for a minute. Maybe now was the time to speak honestly with his father about school. "Actually Dad, I'm going to take a break from my master's program. I think I need some time to figure out what I'm good at and try to really consider what's important to me." Sam looked nervously at his father, "I guess it's about time to think about my future."

Alan listened and was impressed with his own calmness. "Do you have any idea where you want to start?"

"To be honest, I really don't know what I'm looking for or what I might find, so far it's all speculation." Sam continued, "But I want my life to change and to do something worthwhile. I've got some ideas, but I have to decide how to get started."

To Alan, Sam seemed confused and in need of some concrete direction. "Are you interested in working with people or on computers," he inquired.

"I guess both," Sam thought out loud, "with social media you really can't separate the two. I was hoping to get into research, perhaps one-on-one work with a non-profit organization. Even if I started at the bottom of the pile, I know I'm a fast learner."

Alan thought about Carla and the work the center did for teens. He planned to see her in the morning, and he could inquire about a job for Sam. Even if it was only a couple days a week, he would get the feel for that kind of work. In the meantime, he needed more answers from his son.

"Any idea of how long you plan on staying? It's okay with me however long you stay, but at least give me an idea of what you're thinking."

Sam hesitated and then said, "I'm not sure. I need some time to look around and consider the possibilities. But I don't want to get in your way." Sam proceeded cautiously because he didn't have another living arrangement. "Maybe I could help around here, you know, like take Harry for walks and keep real food in the refrigerator," Sam smiled as he chided his father. "I promise to keep things out of your way and not invade your space, even though we have totally different ideas about music and movies." Alan laughed and then mentioned Carla and the work she did at the center. "I could ask her if she had any openings, especially for someone in research."

"Thanks. That would be great! I'll get my résumé ready."

Alan insisted on washing the dishes after dinner and was lingering over the sink when a thought, almost an image, crept through his mind. It was of his father doing dishes after a sumptuous Thanksgiving meal. Alan's mother went to enormous lengths to prepare holiday meals and his father felt his only contribution was to do the dishes. Sometimes this chore took most of the evening.

This picture of his father, made Alan feel nostalgic. Age seemed to be knocking on the door again. He thought sometimes that old age was forever stereotyped. People seemed to deal more with the fear of aging than the experience of old age itself. Alan had always imagined the freedom of the rebellious older years and with it the prospect of making up for the sobriety of youth. When he was young, he considered old age to be one big, funny, wisdom-rich adventure. And yet, people over sixty were constantly talking about various forms of arthritis or comparing their slow impairment of sight and hearing. This kind of vulnerability or sense of loss was unnerving, but because it was gradual, people usually adapted until they realized what was lost.

Is that what Alan was doing? Adapting to old age as it advanced and retreated? Maybe if he just accepted the time-wrought physical and mental changes, he would find some peace. He certainly wanted to avoid the trap of self-pity and the pity of others. Alan's thoughts were not even close to enlightenment as he wiped down the kitchen counters and shook his head wearily. He knew Rose was right, he needed to develop a new lens to see the world and try to get unstuck from old stories so he could create new ones. He sure hoped to change his understanding of aging and to manage his life better.

But whatever stage in his life he was now approaching, he wasn't going to waste time anticipating the finish line. He also reminded himself that he still had his sense of humor and his wits about him, at least for now. Isn't that what everyone wants to hope for?

# TUESDAY, MAY 17<sup>TH</sup>

The next morning, Alan's first stop was to talk with Carla. As he entered her office, it appeared she was absorbed in prayer when he saw her head bowed, and her fingers laced together on her desk. Alan considered her grief to be imposing a certain dignity to the situation they faced. When she finally looked up and saw him standing there, he immediately saw the heart broken look on her face. He tilted his head and nodded to show his complete understanding. He didn't want to pressure her and was aware there were limits to the help she might give to the investigation. Today, Alan only hoped she might share any personal information she knew about Marko.

"Good morning, Carla. I was hoping for a minute to talk some more about Marko."

Carla pondered, "I've been thinking about Marko all morning and struggling to gain some perspective about his life." She offered Alan a chair and continued, "You know, Alan, I always felt a kinship with Marko, but I was also aware that entire landscapes of his past were unknown. Thinking about him now, I believe he wanted it that way."

Carla smiled at Alan and continued, "Marko had such compassion and patience with our teens. He always believed it was easy to judge but more difficult to understand especially when good hearts choose bad methods. He role modeled this with unconditional acceptance and his wonderful ability to easily forgive. That, in a nutshell, was why Marko was so brilliant with the teens."

Carla admired how Marko always let teens talk freely without offering solutions or judgement. "He paid more attention to their thoughts and feelings, and as a result they put their anger aside and became more confident in the process. By empowering teens to confide in him, and to have faith in themselves and their abilities, Marko believed they would make better choices and not have to lean on drugs." Carla shook her head.

Alan leaned in and asked, "Were there any teens Marko worked with who had issues with the center or with Marko?"

"No, there are a few homeless teens, by choice, who think they're owed something from society. These few can become demanding and spiteful and often have to be led out by security." She reached into a folder and handed over their names, but she admitted that she didn't know where to find them.

"Marko did have a problem with a woman on St. Botolph Street," Carla opened a desk drawer and pulled out a file. "She called him a number of times complaining about the noise and frequent comings and goings at the house with the fire. I believe he talked with her at some point." Carla wrote down the woman's name. Alan felt that both leads would help.

He stood and thanked Carla, but then remembered his promise to Sam. "Carla, this may not be the right time to ask, but my son just showed up at my house and is looking for a job. Would you mind talking with him about the center and giving him an idea of non-profit businesses like this?"

Carla agreed and told him to have Sam bring in his résumé. "I'd love to talk to him."

Sidney decided to take the morning off and concentrate on Marko. He admitted his surprise to learn that Marko was a teen-counselor at the Roxbury Teen Center. He thought his brother only belonged to the drag scene all these years. The detective also mentioned that Marko helped him on some cases. Marko's life was more complex than he knew. Wanting to learn more and get involved, Sidney decided to visit the teen center and see if Marko's belongings had to be picked up. Once again, a wave of sadness overcame him.

Carla was surprised to learn that Marko's brother was coming to the center. She wondered why Marko never spoke of having a brother in the city. There wasn't much left on Marko's desk, but she would show Sidney Miller his office space and let him decide what to do with the items. The police had already looked things over and didn't seem too interested.

When Sidney arrived, Carla was struck by how

handsome he was. Marko had been attractive, but Sidney could be a movie star. Maybe it was the way he walked and held himself, but she felt his strength of character and focus. Carla was in her fifties now and was often described as a shoo-in for Octavia Spencer, an actress she admired. Realizing that she was staring at Sidney, she held out her hand to introduce herself.

"I am so sorry for your loss," Carla began, "it must be such a shock for you."

"I appreciate that, Ms. Tompkins, and I hope I won't interfere in any way by being here." Sidney looked carefully at Carla and recognized genuine sadness. Marko had meant something special to this woman. "I have to admit that I wasn't aware of Marko's employment here. Can you tell me about his job at the center, so I can pass it on to my family? We have had little contact with him over the past several years."

Carla asked Sidney to have a seat. Just like the teens she served, she believed families today were so caught up with their own lives that they forgot about the people closest to them. Perhaps the Miller family had reasons to lose touch with Marko, but they had missed out on a lot.

Sidney noticed the curious reaction on Carla's face and continued, "I'm sorry to say that Marko and I were not close. When he left home, Marko wanted complete independence and didn't let any of us know where he was living. I guess we always believed he would come around one day and begin re-connecting with us. I must admit that I'm not in touch often with our family either. Perhaps this will bring us closer."

Carla believed Sidney was sincere in his desire to know more about his brother. She told him about the work the center did and Marko's gift of relating to the teens. Everyone at the center was mourning his death. "You know, Sidney," Carla said, "I believe the only thing that lasts is how we touch people in their hearts, and Marko had such a big heart." Sidney lowered his head with a nod. He was not humble by nature, but something like gratitude for his brother's work flowed from him.

When Carla returned from talking with Sidney, she was surprised to see a young man sitting in her office. Sam immediately stood as she entered and introduced himself. Carla noticed that he was taller than his father but had the same green eyes and kind smile. He handed her his résumé and they sat down to talk.

"Sam," Carla began, "I'm very curious about why you would like to work at a non-profit, especially with teenagers who have troubled pasts. You have obviously been brought up comfortably and have a good education, so what brings you here?"

Sam expected this question and had rehearsed his response. "I believe most people judge others too often on irrelevant reference points, like appearance, lifestyle, and probably even the way we talk. I know I'm guilty of this and I know there's more to life than awesome stuff or social standing." At this point he took a deep breath. "I've come to realize how lucky I've been, the opportunities I've had, and I'd like a chance to pay it forward. I also feel it's time for me to be challenged… as well as gather some experience." Sam looked a little embarrassed and continued, "I remember how confused I was as a teen and how I sometimes balked at people telling me what to do. But I also know how much of a difference all the great support made to my getting ahead. I want to help someone else that way."

Carla's eyebrows raised as she considered this young man. She noticed how nervous he appeared and wondered what experiences he'd had in the college environment. She knew when push came to shove, what the mind wanted, like perspective and acceptance was totally different to what the heart desired, which could be forgiveness and sometimes compassion. Mind and heart were both essential when working with people who needed guidance and acceptance. She wondered just how much Sam wanted to change, or to become more caring about others.

"Sam," Carla asked, "What are you really hoping for?"

"To be happy," Sam sheepishly replied, "just like everyone else, I guess.

Before going to work, Maryanne stared at her reflection in the small mirror over her bathroom sink. Sometimes she looked like her younger self, scared and sad. She had always been a shy, unassuming child growing up beside her seven rambunctious siblings. Her brothers and sisters let her blend easily into their crowded activities and conversations, expecting her to agree without demanding any attention. As a result, Maryanne existed in her world unrecognized, or unseen, even when she tried her best to quietly perform. She was reticent by nature and, therefore, remained invisible, sometimes even to herself.

She always believed there was so much more to life than the small western town where she had grown up. Three years ago, she had married the first guy who asked and moved out of her family home. Maryanne had no idea what a mistake she had made. He was an overbearing drunk and didn't hold back demeaning her in private and in public. He yelled names at her that expressed such hate and ridicule, that it took her breath away. Even when sober, he was never sorry. The one time he hit her, she had gathered her courage and told him she would call the police if it ever happened again.

One day he announced that he had applied to get a master's degree at UMASS in Lowell Massachusetts and they were moving across the country. Maryanne was stunned but felt she had no choice but to go along. They packed as much as was possible into their Buick sedan and began the journey. Maryanne remembered how he drank himself to sleep every night at whatever cheap hotel they stopped at. She had been careful to avoid any conflict and hoped that moving to the East Coast would be an experience to embrace rather than reject.

When they arrived at the small college town, she immediately got a job with a bank. Maryanne loved the people at work and found a kindred friend at the main branch. Betsy was a townie who cringed when Maryanne tried to explain her situation. Betsy immediately saw what a jerk the husband was and set out to remind Maryanne that she had a choice and advised her to leave her despicable husband. Even the employees at the bank became protective of Maryanne and began to despise her husband.

It soon became obvious to Maryanne that she had to end her marriage. Gathering her courage, Maryanne took a day off from work and drove to Boston. She had no idea where to go or what she needed to do, but just the idea of driving away from her problems gave her new energy. The freeway signs directed her to the heart of the city, and she found a parking place in front of Barclay's Bank International. Feeling compelled with her decision to start over, she walked into the bank and applied for a job. Maryanne had been so proud of herself. For the first time in her life, she hadn't told anyone what she was doing so no one could talk her out of it.

A week later she received a call from Barclay's Bank. They wanted to interview her. When she informed her husband that she was leaving, he laughed in her face and said she would never survive in a city like Boston. He reached for his beer and questioned her about where she would live, and he berated her with being afraid of her own shadow. Maryanne grabbed her wallet and walked out the door.

The next day, while her hateful husband was in class, she packed up her belongings and moved out. She was ready for her new life. And that's how she ended up in Boston. Maryanne was surprised how everything fell together once the decision to accept the job at Barclay's was secured. And finding the studio was also a windfall. That had been eight months ago. Everything was going well until now, and Maryanne felt her courage slipping away. She questioned why this fire and, perhaps murder, seemed so personal.

To calm her nerves, Maryanne decided to stop by the

little grocery store at the end of her block and talk things over with Tony, the owner. She knew the St. Botolph Street neighborhood was like family for Tony, and she could easily talk with him about her concerns.

Born to Italian parents, Tony was now in his 70's. His wife had died years ago, and his three children had moved away to find their way in life. In all truth, he told friends, he didn't blame them. In fact, he encouraged them to find their own happiness, but they had to come back for the holidays, which they always did.

Tony often invited neighbors into his shop for wine and cheese on Fridays after work. He enjoyed the company of the younger residents, and they knew he was often filled with local gossip. Tony was proud to say that his family had owned his building since it had been originally built in 1901. Because of his longevity with the area, he was also known to give history lessons about the greater Boston community. Maryanne remembered hearing him say it was an honor that their street was named St. Botolph. The name "Boston" was supposed to be a contraction for Saint Botolph Town.

When Maryanne entered the small shop, she immediately noticed the smell of roasted coffee beans and baked bread. She could feel her shoulders relaxing, and the tension she was feeling beginning to drain away.

"Ahhh... Good morning, Maryanne, my young friend from the wonderful state of Washington." Tony liked to tease Maryanne, as if she were from another country. She appreciated his gentle humor and knew he kept an eye out for her.

Trying to hide the anxiety in her voice, Maryanne asked, "Tony, what have you heard about the fire on our block?"

He looked up and recognized some fear on her face. "I haven't spoken to the police yet, my dear, but it sounds like the building was very badly damaged. I heard someone has perished in the fire, but I don't know who that was."

Tony, as always, wanted to protect Maryanne from any tragedy and try to calm her nerves. She was so young and naïve, and he understood the effort it took for her to try and be a part of things that appeared so easy for everyone else. He also knew how lonely she felt, having no relatives around. Tony hoped she would have the courage to live through the intrusion of a crime investigation on their street.

Tony hesitated to tell Maryanne that the police concluded the cause of the fire was an arson. He did confirm that investigators would be around talking with everyone about what they knew. But Tony reassured Maryanne, "Because you're relatively new to the neighborhood, you probably don't have to worry about being interviewed. If the police do want to talk, just tell them the truth, you don't know anything."

Tony gave a reassuring smile and offered her a wrapped candy that he kept for his customers. He promised to let her know if anything of importance came up.

"Thanks, Tony. I feel unnerved by the whole thing."

As Maryanne walked away, she shuddered at the thought of talking with the police. At least the bank security guards were friendly, but the reputation of the Boston police was filled with misogyny and sexism. Any hostility at all intimidated Maryanne, to the point where she wondered, again, if she had moved to the right city.

"Maryanne!" a voice called out to her. Standing on the short flight of steps in front of an arched entryway, she saw Trudy waving.

"Hi, Trudy, how are you holding up?" Maryanne found out that Trudy had moved to a hotel for a couple weeks while her townhouse was being aired of smoke and to determine if any other damage may have been done to the walls.

"I'm okay, I guess," Trudy sighed, "I just wanted to thank you again for taking my daughter the other night. She was so frightened, and you were the only one close by I could think of to shelter her. I really appreciate your help."

"Have you heard anything about what caused the fire?" Maryanne inquired. "I keep hearing rumors there will be an investigation of arson, at least."

"No, not yet. I have an appointment with a police detective this morning." Trudy turned her head to look down the street. "I hope he gets here soon. He knows I made several calls about that house, and he wants to know why I was so concerned. I'll let you know what I find out."

As Maryanne watched Trudy hurry away down the narrow street, she tried to remember the reasons why Trudy had complained about her neighbors. She knew there was noise on the weekend, but that was understandable in any neighborhood. Could it possibly be more dangerous than just a couple of parties? Who lived there anyway? She would have to ask Tony about this.

# TAKEN BY SURPRISE

Alan stopped at the Starbucks closest to his precinct for his usual bagel and drip coffee. Looking at the names Carla had given him, he began mentally sorting them—immediate interview versus lower priority. He'd already arranged to stop by St. Botolph Street and see the woman who'd kept complaining to Marko. He knew her townhouse was directly adjacent to the destroyed building and had incurred some damage from the fire. If he was lucky, maybe he would catch a few more residents still at home. He grabbed his coffee and was on his way.

Alan parked in front of Trudy's building and stopped for a moment to appreciate the entrance which was decorated with flowing pots of pink and purple flowers. This lovely feminine touch was a sharp contrast to the woman who answered the door. Trudy was tall, around five foot eight, with dark chestnut hair and clear blue eyes. She was dressed completely in black, which highlighted her stunning amber necklace that was surrounded by diamonds. She appeared to be in her thirties and seemed sophisticated in a cold, distant manner.

"Can I help you? I hope you're from the insurance company." Trudy gave an exasperated sigh.

"I'm sorry to hear about the damage to your house," Alan tried to hide his annoyance, "I'm Detective Sharp, I called you earlier to have a few words about the fire next door. Are you comfortable talking here? If not, we can always go somewhere else."

"Oh, Detective, I knew you would be coming by to

talk." Trudy tried to smile. "This is fine. I'm only here to see how the inspection on my building is coming along anyway." With this statement, she opened the door and escorted Alan into the entrance of her building.

The first floor was a rented studio space, and so they continued up the stairs. There appeared to be two apartments on the second floor and Trudy's was the door on the left. Entering the living room, Trudy swept aside two layers of plastic that were covering her tan leather sofa and asked Alan to have a seat. The sofa dominated the room and faced an exposed brick wall that housed a floor to ceiling fireplace. The room itself was a popular open design with the large kitchen, dining and living space, all connected. The hardwood floors and high ceilings made the room look much larger than it probably measured. Alan noticed some attempts had been made to update the counters but could also see that the appliances were out of date and the floors needed recoating.

Trudy seated herself and tried to explain, "I'm waiting to hear from the insurance people so I can get started on all the work that needs to be done. There's extensive smoke damage to every room."

"Do you live here alone?"

Trudy frowned and shifted uncomfortably. "I share custody of my daughter. She stays with me sometimes."

"Was she with you on the night of the fire?" Alan noticed how nervous this lady was becoming and wondered what she was hiding.

Trudy fidgeted with her necklace and took a deep breath. "If you must know, she's only three years old and she lives with her father. Yes, she was here that night, but when I heard the fire engines and smelled the smoke, I rushed her to a neighbor's house."

Alan jotted down some notes and then looked up at Trudy, "Then what did you do?"

"I waited! The police and fire people warned us all to stay outside. Why are you questioning me?" Trudy crossed her arms.

Alan refused to acknowledge her irritation and continued, "I understand you've made several complaints about the building next door, the one with the fire, for quite some time," Alan sat up a bit straighter, "could you give me an idea what the problems were?"

Trudy looked up towards the ceiling, as if the answers were written in the air, and finally started listing her complaints. "Strange teenagers were coming and going at all hours of the day. There were noisy parties and loud music was playing late into the night. I'm pretty certain drugs and alcohol were involved." She stopped and looked at Alan directly, "I've gone over there a couple of times to ask them to be respectful of the neighbors, but the kids who were there just laughed and started throwing things. When I called the police, things settled down for a while. But lately, it has escalated again, and I even noticed older people joining the group."

"Did you know Marko Miller?" Alan asked.

"Yes, I met him one day while taking a walk. He was having a serious conversation with a young teen, cautioning him about hanging around with the wrong crowd. He was obviously involved in some way with the kid. I had seen him in

78

the area before, chatting with some of the local Black kids. So, I figured, of all people, you know, he might do something about the drugs being sold at that address."

Recognizing the obvious racial profiling, Alan was even more annoyed by this woman. Now he knew why her complaints to the police were largely ignored. Trudy continued, "Marko mentioned that he worked at the Roxbury Teen Center and knew a great deal about drug abuse and problems teens were up against. So, when things got really bad, I called the center and asked for his help."

Trudy said she liked Marko. "I felt confident that he would listen to me and do what he could to help. Is it true that he's the one who died in the fire?"

"I'm afraid so." Alan looked at Trudy to see how she would respond.

Trudy stared at him and finally said, "I'm sorry to hear that."

"Did you see any drug dealing going on in that building or on the street?"

"Well, not really, Detective. I just assumed all the noise and partying was drug related. Wouldn't you?"

Alan looked down at his notebook to hide his annoyance. "One more question, do you know the name of anyone who lived in that building?"

Trudy gave a small laugh, "Of course not, they all seemed rather young and needy to me. And I try to keep to myself."

Alan left Trudy and wondered first, how honest she was about her dealings with Marko, and secondly, how she could afford to live in such an expensive building. She and her husband had purchased it years ago, but they were now divorced, and she only worked at a department store. Perhaps she had family money.

Trudy had secrets she carefully guarded for most of her adult life. So long, in fact, that it had become a habit. She believed if she made up a story and seemed convincing, no one really cared about finding out the truth. Her lying had become an art form. As a precaution, though, she always stuck as close to the truth as possible and pretended to volunteer facts that were carefully selected for effect. Although her lies were believable to most people, she feared they would soon catch up to her now that the police were involved. Trudy had lied about knowing Marko. She had been keeping an eye on him once she found out he was working at the teen center. She was afraid he might have found out about her own little business.

Trudy had started selling drugs in college. In the beginning, it was just party pills and it helped finance her school tuition. When she left school and moved to Boston, she realized that everyone she met was taking some sort of upper or downer. At first, she easily made a few small sales to co-workers and customers at work as a way to supplement her lousy pay. But after a while, she realized the demand grew with the availability, so she quietly expanded her sales network. Over time, the buying and selling of drugs continued to prove very profitable for Trudy. When she learned to follow the rules of smooth operations, she cleared over $200,000 per annum. She had a well-connected supplier, of course, and only sold to carefully selected clients. Trudy was savvy and smart, and she knew the police only caught the dumb ones.

Lately, however, Trudy was frustrated by having to compete with younger sellers who were quickly diminishing her quality of business. It was not a contest she wanted to lose, but she also realized she had enough money to begin again somewhere new. Perhaps her only safe option now was to leave the city.

As part of her divorce settlement, Trudy saw her daughter on various weekends when it could be arranged. As a part-time mother, she knew she sometimes took chances with her responsibilities. She hadn't meant to leave her sleeping child alone at home on the night of the fire, but she'd had to meet with a drug contact. It was supposed to be a short meeting to finalize an agreement and hand over some customers. When she returned home and heard the commotion of the street, she had rushed into her building to hear Clara screaming. Panicked and unable to know what to do first, Trudy grabbed her daughter and ran for help. Once her ex found out about this, he would finally get full custody. She realized her three-year-old Clara was never going to stay with her again, she was positive of this outcome.

Trudy decided to plan her escape quickly and carefully so she would be free to leave town as soon as the insurance money came through. She already had a plane ticket and $25,000 in cash stored in a safety deposit box. She would put the building in her ex-husband's name and fly to Cabo. When it sold, he could keep the equity for himself and Clara. She didn't need any of the profit because she had enough money in an offshore account to last her for years. She just wanted to disappear. Her first stop would be to a Mexican time share her friend owned so she could collect her thoughts and relax. She had been there many times before and enjoyed the weather, food and entertainment. Nobody in her everyday life knew of this friend, so she was certain she wouldn't be located. Trudy had a burner phone and a new email account. Her ticket said she was going to San Diego, which was true. But from there she was booked on a cruise liner to Cabo with another passport. The secrets she had guarded for so long added to her belief that no one wanted to know the truth about her anyway.

Alan left Trudy and walked along St. Botolph Street, wondering if he might catch someone still at home. As he strolled, he noticed how perfectly the individual buildings related to each other and gave a unified appearance to the street. This street had the feeling of intimacy and charm, like a grandmother who you love. His father had always marveled how architectural styles, even when generally mixed, still had wonderful integrity and created warmth.

As he arrived at the end of the block, he noticed a young woman waiting at the crosswalk.

"Excuse me, miss," Alan called, "do you live around here?" He stopped and waited for an answer.

Already late for work, Maryanne was taken by surprise and jumped slightly. She had been lost in thought and didn't see this man approach.

"Yes, I do," she muttered and looked at her watch. "Can I help you with something?"

Alan took out his ID and said that he was the detective handling the case of the house that burned the other night. "I was just talking with your neighbor, Trudy, and wondered if you were home the night of the fire."

Maryanne hesitated and then said, "Yes. Trudy brought her daughter to me while she ran back to her building. I really have to get to work, I'm running late."

Alan quickly described Marko and asked if she knew him.

"No, I don't know him. I'm sort of new to the neighborhood and don't know a lot of people." Maryanne nervously clutched her bag as if for protection.

"Where do you work?" Alan smiled, trying to reassure her that she could relax.

"At Barclay's Bank in town," Maryann replied with a timid smile. Alan noted that this young woman was trying her best to hide the anxiety in her voice, and he felt a tinge of protectiveness for some reason.

"Sorry to keep you. Please let me know if you hear anything unusual or if you have any questions," Alan handed his card to her. "We'll be around the neighborhood interviewing people, hoping someone saw anything that could help us with the case. The man who died in the fire was a good guy, and a friend of mine." Alan thought he saw sadness enter her face and he wondered how old she was. He politely nodded and watched her walk away.

Alan continued through the St. Botolph neighborhood, knocking on a few doors, but found no one home. He wondered how much rent was charged for the apartments in these buildings and how much time people spent at home. Because of inflation, not to mention all the extra expenses like rising health care, car insurance, and internet costs, who had time to relax? Just as he pondered this conundrum, his cellphone rang, and Alan was surprised to see Sidney's name appear.

"Hello, Detective, I was hoping we might arrange to meet at Marko's condo tomorrow or sometime soon. I'd like to have a look around and see if I can put some things in order for him." Sidney sounded tentative and Alan wondered how difficult this was going to be for him. Marko's death must be weighing heavily.

"Sure, I can meet in the morning around nine. I'm meeting with the manager to get the key then. Did I give you the address?"

"Yes, you did. Thank you." The formality in Sidney's voice caused Alan to imagine how impressive he must be in court.

Looking at his watch, Alan decided to drive to the precinct and make some phone calls while reviewing his notes. Two days into the case and he felt at sea. When he got to his desk, he saw he had a few phone messages. Once an investigation became public, he knew people of all sorts called in saying that they could help, or even wanting to turn themselves in. He usually let the other officers respond to these calls and only forward possible leads on to him.

However, one of the calls on his desk looked interesting. The note said that a woman called with information about Marko. Her name was Alicia Grant and Marko had worked for her. Alan immediately called the number and left a message on voicemail. Hopefully, she would call him back before he left for the day.

Alan knew he was a good detective. He had worked years to learn strong critical thinking, as well as problem-solving skills, and had learned through experience that interviews were often the cornerstone of all investigations. He looked for the gaps in a story and read body language well. That was why he had a problem with Trudy. She was a little too distant, her emotions too controlled. She was hiding something, he didn't know what, but his instincts told him she knew more than she was saying—maybe a lot more.

Why would she lie to him? Alan mentally weighed the possibilities: Trudy was protecting someone; she wanted to avoid punishment; to maintain privacy; to obtain financial benefit; or to have power over someone. She lived next door to the damaged building and could gain monetarily from a fire. In fact, she said she was hoping he was from the insurance company. Maybe she and the owner of the other building were in this together. Alan knew he had to wait until Monday to talk with the other owner, David Reagan, and hear his story. He put his thoughts on hold and spent the rest of the day writing reports and documenting what he knew so far in the investigation.

# TAKEN BY SURPRISE

Alan finally walked in the door of his house around six and was greeted by the spicey smells of Mexican cooking. Sam was surprising him again with his exUberance in the kitchen.

"Whatever you're making, I'll have seconds," Alan smiled. "How did it go with Carla today"

Sam offered his dad a beer and sat down at the counter. "Actually, I don't really know. She's an awesome lady, and I think I'd really like working for her, but she gave me some things to think about."

"That sounds like Carla," Alan took a sip of his beer. "She runs an impressive operation and needs people who are dedicated and willing to put in the time and energy for things to work. Their clients are challenging. Did she ask you about grant writing?" Alan knew his son was very good at this.

"Yes. When she found out my degree was focused on research, she asked if I had ever reached out to foundations for money. I told her I was familiar with the basics of professional grant writing: contact, research, and discussion, write, submit, and follow up. That's how I was able to get funding for my independent studies over the years."

"So, what did she ask you to think about?" Alan wondered.

"She asked me to write her a letter and state what I was looking for, what I was afraid of, and what kind of help I wanted or needed from her. She also asked me to tell her something that others may be surprised to know about me. And, just between you and me, I'm embarrassed to admit I've never really thought seriously about that stuff. It's kind of humbling." Sam took a drink of beer, realizing that talking helped formulate his thoughts. "So far in my life, I've been lucky, I guess. But I don't really have a plan; I've just tried to take advantage of opportunities as they presented themselves. I'll be working on the letter tonight."

While they ate a hearty meal of beef enchiladas, Alan reassured Sam that being challenged to think in new ways was all a part of growing and learning. Even if a job with Carla wasn't the right fit, he knew Sam would get some good advice from her.

Alan wondered to himself if Sam recognized how his privileged life might stymie his decision. Brought up by well-to-do parents, in an upper-class environment, he'd experienced the world within a fairly narrow framework. Even his college and grad school experience had been largely focused on other people like himself. If he were to work at the Teen Center, he would quickly learn that life was more complicated and much more challenging to most people.

On the other hand, Alan found himself a little envious of Sam's enthusiasm. He wished he could reclaim some of the youthful enthusiasm his son was showing. When this investigation was over, he would try to stop just drifting through life and become more proactive in setting and meeting goals for himself. After all, he wasn't too old to learn new tricks, as the advertising goes. Well, he reminded himself as he caught his reflection in the kitchen window, at least he was blessed with beautiful white teeth and a youthful complexion due to the Vitamin E oil he used daily. He smiled.

# WEDNESDAY, MAY 18<sup>TH</sup>

Alan understood and appreciated Sidney's request to be allowed into Marko's condo, and he also thought having a family member present could help clear up any questions that might arise. For instance, Sidney might be able to explain who got what from Marco's estate if he hadn't left a will. Over the years, Alan had seen many battles erupting over sentimental and monetary possessions. He wondered what they would find now.

Marko's condo was in an older, downtown neighborhood across from the Rose Kennedy Greenway. The young manager greeted Alan and pointed to Sidney who was waiting by the elevators. He had already introduced himself and was holding a key to the condo. Alan wondered if Sidney always wanted to be a step ahead or if his curiosity about his brother was beginning to show.

Stepping into the condo, they immediately realized that Marko was a collector. Dark wood bookcases filled the entire living area wall and appeared to be dedicated to travel books and mysteries. But the most surprising discovery was the collection of exotic animal statues that were scattered throughout the house. Large and small, these statues must have been pricey because they were so life-like. Alan stood in wonder at the beautiful Hyacinth Macaw that stared down at him. Its length was almost a meter with a long and pointed tail. The feathers were a vibrant blue and the ring around the parrot's eyes and under the beak were a bright yellow. It was extraordinary. Sidney seemed equally entranced with the lynx that crouched near the kitchen. The large, padded paws and long whiskers were accentuated by the animal's beige-white fur coloring. Under the neck there was a ruff of black fur resembling a bow tie. Other creatures crawled or lurked around the room. It was both fascinating and alarming.

Looking for a computer, Alan noticed a desk in the corner. A closed laptop was obvious along with unpaid bills and blank envelopes. When Alan opened the laptop, he saw it was protected with a password as expected. He would have to take it with him. Sidney was in the kitchen opening cupboards and whistling. Apparently, Marko had plenty of appliances and cookbooks.

Alan surveyed the one-bedroom space with growing interest. The hardwood floors and modern kitchen contrasted with an old comfortable velvet sofa and love seat. The few pictures on the walls were professional photos of jungles and rain forests that set the stage for the wild animals in the collection. Marko was beginning to seem a much more adventurous person. Alan missed him.

Spending almost an hour looking for any clues or signs, Alan noticed the time on the antique clock near the door and was ready to depart. "I can't find anything else of use, Sidney, but I'm taking the laptop back to the precinct to search through it. Are you going to stay?"

Sidney looked up from the stack of books he had taken down from the shelves, "I'm going to spend a little more time here. I want to get some photos of the statues and books and send them to my family. We should decide as a group how to deal with it all." Because he was single, and local, Sidney didn't mind being the one to take charge.

Sidney walked Alan out to his car in order to get his briefcase and camera. On his way back inside, he was stopped by a woman standing outside Marko's apartment.

"Hi, I'm Lily. Are you looking for Marko?" The woman seemed interested and eager for conversation. "Because he's not here. I've been trying to get ahold of him, but he doesn't answer his phone." She was young, around thirty, with cinnamon brown skin and bright hazel eyes. She was dressed in designer jeans and a stylish overcoat and leaned casually against the apartment door.

"I'm his brother," Sidney hesitantly replied. "I'm sorry to tell you that Marko has died. I'm here to go through his things." Stopping a minute to wonder what to say next, Sidney asked, "Did you know him well?"

Letting out an uncontrollable sob, she cried, "What happened? Was there an accident? The last time I saw him he was fine, and we were planning on going to a movie this week!" Lily's face registered her shock. "Dead?" she said in disbelief. "How? When?" Tears began to flow down her face. She swiped them away and then held up her hand unsteadily. She gulped, took a ragged breath, and exhaled. Fighting to keep control, she stepped away from the door and sighed, "Can we talk later?" Using an envelope she was carrying, she wrote down her phone number, handed it to Sidney, and slowly walked away.

Lily had met Marko when she moved into the building a year ago. The condo she stayed in was owned by her Aunt Sheila who had recently died. Lily had been asked by the family to live there and take care of the place until the estate was finalized. Because her aunt had failed to write a will, there were a nightmare of arguments brewing for months over her personal items and property. Lily secretly hoped the bickering would continue because she loved the condo and her aunt's eccentric treasures. Even Marko liked to visit and look through Aunt Sheila's years of travel photos on weekends. Lily could not grasp the thought that he was dead.

Sidney sat on the velvet sofa and wondered if he should let Detective Sharp know about Lily. Maybe if he found something of importance in his further search, he would include her in the conversation. He took out his camera and began to photograph Marko's collections. There were four larger animal statues and several smaller ones. He also looked through the kitchen cupboards and drawers and took some photos of the larger appliances. Did Marko cook? The rice cooker and Kitchen Aid mixer looked very well used, and so did the Wok. He had silver and dishes for twelve, along with beverage and wine glasses. Did he entertain? Sidney was beginning to feel sorry that he didn't know more about Marko's social life.

Everything was going smoothly until Sidney heard the doorbell ring. At the door was Lily again, this time with a package addressed to Marko.

"When Marko isn't home, I usually pick up his mail," Lily explained.

This time, Sidney insisted that Lily stay for a cup of tea or coffee and help him to understand more about his brother. She hesitated, and then stepped into the room.

"Marko loved these statues," Lily reached for the blue sea turtle that was exquisitely sculpted. "Every time he bought one, he would have a dinner party and introduce his new animal. It was silly, but also sweet. I always teased him that he probably had pet names for each one, but he would just laugh. He said they kept him company." She carefully placed the animal back on the desk where she found it.

"Do you know the names of his friends?" Sidney asked. "Because I would like to let them know about his death. Maybe he has an address book somewhere, but I haven't found it yet."

"Marko kept everything on his phone." Lily put her hand to her mouth and gasped, "Has anyone told Jerome about Marko's death? He's Marko's best friend!"

"I don't really know if he's been contacted. Do you have a number for Jerome?"

"No," Lily looked worried, "but I think you might find him at the club. The Dragonfly Theater I mean. Marko designed dresses for all the guys. He was amazing... they're going to be devastated!"

Lily turned to leave but then pointed to the package she had delivered. "It's probably another animal statue." The box was small, and once they decided to open it, they found a wallet inside. It was Marko's. Quickly dropping the box, Sidney reached for his phone to call Detective Sharp.

When his cellphone rang, Alan was just pulling into the police station. Sidney Miller sounded upset. He was still at Marko's apartment and said he had a package that had been delivered by a neighbor. Inside was Marko's wallet. Alan immediately turned his car around and changed his course of the day.

Sidney and Lily were waiting at the door when Alan arrived. Quick introductions were made, and Alan was led into the living room. There on the sofa was an opened box with a wallet inside.

"Where did you find this package, Lily?" Alan asked.

"Our building packages are always left at the desk or by our doors. When I walked into the building after work yesterday, the manager said there was a package for Marko because he knew I would take it to him. Marko relied on me because he didn't want anything to get lost. When I saw Mr. Miller here today and found out Marko was dead, I brought the package to him." Becoming overwhelmed again with all that was happening, Lily started to cry. She collapsed into the velvet chair and hid her face in her hands.

Putting on protective gloves, Alan picked up the wallet and looked through it. Marko's license, debit card, and Visa card were there along with some cash. There was also a picture of an older Black couple that Sidney identified as their parents. Sidney turned away for a minute to compose himself. Alan took out a plastic bag and put the box and wallet into it. He would take it in for fingerprints, but he assumed it had been wiped down. Especially if the person who sent it had something to do with Marko's death.

"Have you spoken to Jerome yet?" Lily asked Alan.

"No, I haven't. Who's Jerome?"

"He's Marko's best friend in the world! He runs the drag shows where Marko works designing the gowns. He's going to be shattered!"

Alan felt he was possibly making progress in a small way. He would find Jerome and talk with him. But he wondered why someone would send Marko's wallet through the mail. It was probably just someone who found it and was being a good citizen. Alan took down Lily's information and, once again, headed for his office.

Trudy was irritated. The insurance company who handled her property was not approving the claim she sent to them. Apparently, arson required a hold on processing that would delay any payout, and consequently, the work she had planned for her building. Everything in her place needed to be updated, and she was hoping the insurance payout would cover the cost to remodel the apartment before listing the place. When she and her ex bought the building, they didn't have enough ready cash to modernize floors and kitchens like the other wealthy owners on the block. She hoped to use the insurance money to update her place and prep it for sale.

Desperate to know how the arson investigation was going, Trudy walked to the end of the block to talk with Tony. She didn't like how curious, or nosey, he was about everyone who lived in the neighborhood, but this time he could be of use.

"Good morning, Tony," Trudy greeted, "How are you today?" She walked over to the coffee bar and helped herself to a cup. Trying to keep it casual, she smiled slightly and asked, "Have you heard anything about the investigation into the fire last weekend?"

Tony looked up from his broom with disgust. He never liked Trudy because of her cold, condescending manner. He always liked her ex-husband and had been delighted when they split. Tony admired the courage it took him to walk away and not become trapped by her selfishness and bitterness. It made him smile to himself.

"What investigation?" Tony glared at Trudy.

"Oh, come on, Tony. Have you heard anything about who might have committed the arson? I spoke briefly with the detective in charge, and he wasn't very helpful. The work on my building has been delayed because there appears to be an ongoing investigation. I just want to know if you've heard how long it's going to take."

It was difficult for Tony to believe that a person could be this indifferent about such a tragedy as someone losing their life. Trudy had not even mentioned the fact that Marko had died. She was heartless. In fact, this seemed more like hostility than indifference to him. "I don't know anything,"

Tony said and walked quickly behind the counter, leaving Trudy to figure things out on her own. Disappointed with his response, she took her coffee and left.

A few minutes later another St. Botolph Street resident walked into the store. Tony rose from the old stool behind the till and held out his hand to greet him. If Tony noticed the worried appearance in Ron's eyes, he didn't show it.

"Hello, Ron, good to see you." This will be interesting, Tony considered silently, especially if he wants to talk about the fire, too.

Ron was a short man with thinning hair, a sharp nose, and skinny dark rimmed glasses. He frequently came across as self-important, despite his stature, and his voice was demanding in tone, as if he were being persecuted daily. Ron was the self-appointed block watch captain for the neighborhood, which gave him the authority he relished.

"Tony, how's business?"

"Business is always good," Tony replied with an amused self-assurance. Because he was interested in why Ron was there, he didn't ask the usual friendly questions. Tony waited.

Ron cleared his throat with authority. "I'm worried about the street's drug problem, Tony. In fact, the community board members and I met last night and wondered about the investigation of the fire at the end of the block. What can you tell me?"

Tony knew that Ron was only interested in the present and immediate danger for the community. He noticed, once again, there was no mention of the sad tragedy that someone had died in the fire. He appeared to only need reassurance that something was being done.

Careful to not offer an opinion, Tony replied, "I haven't heard much, actually. The police are interviewing people in the neighborhood. Have they spoken to you?"

Ron shook his head negatively. "I would be happy to talk with them any time. Lately, I've been keeping a list of unfamiliar cars that drive by regularly. I know this is a popular neighborhood, but sometimes it's good to keep track of things."

Tony couldn't imagine what Ron might be looking for, or what he was hoping to find, so he continued to remain neutral and not express an opinion.

Another customer entered the store, interrupting the conversation between the two men. As Ron walked out, Tony wondered if he should inform Detective Sharp about Ron's list of transient cars the neighborhood.

Sam was working on his letter to Carla. He was fully aware of the comforts and opportunities he took for granted and knew his life had been much easier than the people she helped each day.

Sam grew up traveling from house to house after his parents were divorced. He was eight at the time and tried to make the best of both worlds. When his father remarried a few years later, Sam became more self-contained. He did well in school and had some friends, but life was confusing at times. All he wanted to do was play video games and keep to the joint custody schedule the adults negotiated for him. If he complained, everyone felt depressed, and he hated that more than getting his way. Although he was lonely at times, Sam concentrated on his future and dreamed of moving far away.

As soon as he completed his high school senior year, Sam was accepted at UCLA. The campus was thousands of miles from home and that fact alone gave him the freedom and reassurance he longed for. But his faith in himself, such as it was, was a fragile thing. He had a lot of growing up to do. Sam fell into the trap that far too many college students give in to. He started taking pills to stay awake and study, wanting desperately to compete with students who appeared much smarter. Taking drugs like Ritalin and Adderall made Sam feel more confident and helped him manage his anxiety. By the time he graduated from college, he had a problem.

Sam was clever enough to gather sufficient scholarship and grant money and continue to grad school. He tried to stop taking the drugs he relied on, but the withdrawal symptoms were unmanageable. The anxiety was overwhelming. He also realized he had developed a significant tolerance level to drugs and worried when he needed a higher dose to get the desired effect. Sam was constantly afraid, waiting for the moment when someone might discover the truth about his addiction.

That was why he ended up in Boston. Sam knew the drugs had a hold on him and he needed help. It was time to begin a better life, one that allowed him to be drug free, and yet keep optimistic in the process. Otherwise, his future looked unsettled.

Sam hadn't seen his father in a couple of years and hoped he could get up the courage to confide in him. But because he was working on a new case, Alan was mostly unavailable. Sam's next thought was that Carla would be the obvious person to help him. She wanted to know what Sam was afraid of, and he wondered if she had already spotted him as a guy on drugs. This was becoming more complex.

As he wrote the letter Carla expected, he thought he might allude to the drugs available in college and that he had tried some. He wanted Carla to know about the social pressures prevalent on college campuses and the relentless competition. Sam also intended to tell her about his goals for a meaningful future. But he knew whatever he longed for like security, recognition, respect, and a successful career, were completely out of his grasp until he got a better grip on his drug dependence. What he was most afraid of, was failure.

Frustrated by not setting up interviews earlier, Alan stopped to get his regular coffee and sandwich at the deli. He needed something to eat now if he was going to stay late at the office and finally begin analyzing this case. Things were seldom as they appear, Alan reminded himself, and he needed time to plot out the facts he did know and then maybe understand what he still needed to find out. This was the point in any case, when people and events either come together to paint a picture or remain a mystery that needs to be solved.

Alan was met by his lieutenant when he walked through the precinct door. "Alan, I need an update on your investigation. We've received a number of calls already, the insurance company for the building and the owner's lawyer who's called about three times."

Alan was unnaturally annoyed and raised his hand in acknowledgement. Trying to keep his temper at bay, he told his boss about the search of Marko's condo, leaving out the package containing his wallet. Wanting to be left alone for a while, Alan said he was going to set up an information timeline and would have more ideas later in the day.

"By the way," his boss raised his eyebrows in a suggestive way, "there's an interesting couple waiting for you who say they have information about Marko Miller."

Walking into his office, Alan tried to hide his amusement when he saw a woman sitting beside his desk next to a colorfully attired man who was dressed in a bright Hawaiian shirt, rolled up jeans and a green leather jacket. He appeared to be wearing make-up. The woman surprised Alan by immediately jumping out of her chair and holding out her hand to greet him.

"Detective, I'm Alicia Grant and I just found out about Marko."

Alan took her hand and invited her to sit once more. He was struck by how her very presence brightened the dull room. She was tall, around 5'9", and was wearing a mauve woven skirt with tassels hanging from the hem, a bright yellow tank top, and western boots. Her long auburn hair was angled on one side but fell forward attempting to hide her darting hazel eyes. She was thin and could have just stepped out of a photo shoot Alan thought. Her facial features were strong, full bright tangerine lips, a dramatic long sculptured nose, and her eyes, outlined in coal, stared intently at Alan.

"And I'm Jerome," said the teary man, "I'm just devastated to learn that my best friend in the entire world has died." He stayed seated and patted away tears that had fallen onto his jacket.

"Let me begin with you, Miss Grant, tell me, how did you know Marko?"

Alicia gave a long sigh. She picked up her bag, shaped like a carpetbag his mother always admired, and rummaged for a brochure of her store. "I own the Mystic Lady shop in town. My clients are interested in unique, edgy, one-of-a-kind designs. I opened my business several years ago and was amazed when I soon had more customers than I could deal with. I needed to find someone to help me before things got out of my control. Let me tell you, Detective, there are a lot of wealthy women in Boston."

At this point she handed Alan a stylish pamphlet outlining her store services. "Anyway," she continued, "I saw Marko's gowns for the drag queens, thanks to Jerome I might add, and asked him to join me. Marko worked part time at my shop for the past two years. He was one of my best designers. I just cannot believe he's dead!" She pulled a handkerchief out of her bag and dabbed her eyes.

"When was the last time you saw Marko?"

"Last week. We were busy with two clients who are very demanding and needed their orders filled ASAP." Alicia paused and took a breath as she absently played with the beautiful turquoise stone on her beaded necklace. "Any time that Marko could spare for me was appreciated. I never understood how he kept up with all he had on his plate. I know he worked part time at the teen center, and designed the drag dresses, and then put up with me." Alicia looked sheepishly at Alan. "I'm difficult."

Alan momentarily tried to imagine how difficult she might be, but then turned back to the investigation. "How did he seem when you saw him last week?"

"Great! He was looking forward to a big drag show with Jerome because several of his gowns were chosen. Marko was a genius dressing those guys. I think they loved him as much as the gowns."

Alan looked at Jerome, who was attempting to stop his tears. "When was the last time you saw Marko?"

Jerome adjusted himself in his chair to give his full attention to Alan. His crossed legs and his pointed glossy shoes were swinging at a rapid pace. "That was the show, at the Dragonfly Theater, Alicia was just mentioning. Marko and I went to the show together and then we went out for drinks afterward. Can you please just tell me what happened to him? Was he really in that horrible fire?"

"I'm afraid he was. Jerome. When did you last talk with Marko?"

"On Friday night. We had a bit too much to drink and not enough food at the restaurant… the Ritz by the way. Poor Marko got wasted, and I had to put him in an Uber to make sure he got home okay. That was the last time I saw him."

Alicia pulled out a pack of cigarettes while Jerome wiped away more tears.

Alan shook his head towards Alicia. "Sorry, not in here. Can I get you a cup of coffee or some water?"

Alicia put the cigarette away, stood and looked around. "I can get it myself if you show me where to go."

Amused and a little taken aback, Alan walked her to the staff kitchen and motioned to the mugs and water glasses. "Whatever you decide."

Taking water back to the office for Jerome and herself, Alicia quietly asked, "What exactly happened to dear Marko? All I heard was that he was killed in a fire."

"The fire on St. Botolph Street Saturday night appears to be arson and we know that Marko died in the fire."

"Are you telling me that Marko set the fire?" Alicia's eyes were boring holes into Alan.

"No. I believe Marko was a victim of this fire. We're investigating why he was there and how he could have died. Do either of you have any idea who would want to hurt him?"

Jerome looked at Alan with a stunned expression, "No one would ever hurt Marko!"

Alicia agreed, "I can't imagine anyone wanting to hurt him. He was a wonderful person who everyone loved. What can we do to help you?"

Alan was surprised with this offer. They both appeared determined to be a part of this investigation. He was slightly puzzled by what they meant by wanting to help. What did either of them possibly know about helping with an on-going homicide investigation? They were an odd couple in more ways than one Alan concluded.

"Leave me your phone numbers and I will get back to

you. As we gather more information, I may want to speak with you again."

Jerome handed Alan his business card which was bright orange and red. He then tried to compose himself as he stood and walked out the door.

Alicia stood and looked directly into Alan's eyes and said, "I am not going to let this go, Detective. I want answers because I owe it to Marko. In fact, my clients are going to be very upset to learn about his death. And some of them are the elite of Boston. I will let you know if I hear anything peculiar or of interest from one of them."

At this point Alicia handed her empty glass to Alan as she rifled through her bag and brought out her colorful business card. "I'll be in touch." As Alan watched her walk out of his office, he envied Marko's relationship with such a dynamic woman.

Alan turned his attention to the incident board that dominated one wall of his office. He taped Marko's photo on it and below it listed some information: name, age, address, place of work, and time of death. He wrote Sidney's name next to Marko's as his nearest relative and Lily's name as a contact. He also listed Carla's name and number along with the St. Botolph Street address where Marko had been found. Looking at the information his lieutenant had handed him, he wrote the name David Regan who was the owner of the burnt building. He then noted the name and number of Les Quinn, the insurance company representative who had called. Last of all, Alan taped Alicia's and Jerome's cards to the board.

Now Alan needed to review the teenagers who

worked with Marko. Carla had noted that three of the young people were under sixteen and would have to be interviewed with a parent or a guardian. The other seven were older, but four of those teens had not been keeping their regular appointments for a couple of weeks. Listing the ten names of the teens on the white board, Alan made notes from Carla's information and decided to begin calling the three names that were easiest to contact.

Kyle Rosen was 18 years old and lived with his father in South Roxbury. He was completing his GED at the local community college and worked at a gas station a few days a week. When Alan called Kyle's cell, he was surprised that he answered so quickly. Alan introduced himself and asked if Kyle knew about Marko.

"Yeah," Kyle mumbled. "I heard. Damn shame. He was a good guy."

"When was the last time you saw him?" Alan inquired.

"I don't really remember," Kyle quietly said, "maybe last week sometime. We have our regular meetings on Tuesdays, so I guess that was it. I'm really bummed to know he is dead."

Alan asked Kyle if he could meet him at his job for a quick interview. Kyle said he would rather come to the precinct, and they set an appointment for the next morning. Next on the list was Eddie Pearson, who was a senior at the local high school. When Alan called his cell, it went immediately to voicemail and so he left a message. Bret Grisham was the final call he made. Bret worked at Starbucks and, after agreeing to speak with Alan, asked if they could meet somewhere besides the precinct. They agreed to meet at a café in the city.

Reviewing the other seven profiles, Alan decided to call Carla again and ask her opinion about the youngest three. He was reluctant to interfere with any progress Marko had made with them and wondered if they were assigned another counselor. Maybe he could start by talking to the professionals.

When Alan finally got ahold of Carla, she had just finished reading the email from Sam. She was impressed with his honesty and wondered if Alan knew what was written. She decided to hire Sam if he could start immediately, but she was bound by confidentiality and couldn't discuss this with Alan. Out of respect and courtesy, she would let father and son confide in each other.

Impressed with Alan's progress, Carla reviewed each client of Marko's with him. She had doubts about any one of them being involved with his death, but she understood Alan's need to track down potential clues and persons of interest in every case. As a friend, Carla asked him to keep her informed.

# THURSDAY, MAY 19<sup>TH</sup>

Kyle Rosen and his father, Steve, were waiting for Alan when he entered his office the next morning. Both men were Black and built like line backers. Steve looked young enough to pass for Kyle's older brother, and Alan was impressed he had accompanied his son to the precinct.

"Why are we here?" Steve began, "Is this about Marko Miller? My son is devastated that he died." Kyle interrupted his father, "Why do you want to talk to me? Marko and I were friends. He was helping me get my life in order."

Alan understood their concerns and worries. Whenever a Black person was asked to come in for questioning, it was assumed, without any proof or evidence, they were guilty. He hated this about society and hoped he might be able to reassure these two men he was not accusing them of anything. "Please understand, I only want to talk with Kyle about the last time he spoke with Marko, to get a sense of what Marko was doing the days before his death. You had a meeting with him on Tuesday, is that right, Kyle?"

"Yeah, we talked. He was cool about my job and school. We did a kind of schedule or what he called a timeline to get me through to graduation. I have it here if you want to see it."

Alan appreciated the gesture and looked over the plan Marko had made for Kyle. He smiled and gave it back to the worried teen, hoping he would relax. "Did you plan to meet again?"

"Yeah. We meet every Tuesday. Marko said he would be talking to my boss and teachers to give them a good report on my progress. He said everything looked okay, I didn't have to worry about anything."

Steve looked concerned and put his hand on his son's shoulder. "What happened to Marko anyway? How did he die? All we heard was that there was a fire, and he was in the building. Can you tell us anymore?"

Alan shook his head, "I wish I could. Right now, it's an ongoing investigation." Alan looked hopefully at Kyle, "Were you at work on Saturday night?" Alan was trying his best not to appear accusing.

"Yes, I worked until 11:00," Kyle replied. "Then I went home because I had an early shift in the morning." Steve confirmed this.

Alan gave them his card and thanked them for coming in. As he watched them walk out, he once again blamed himself and society for holding people accountable just because of the color of their skin. He could read the distrust and worry in both men's eyes and felt powerless and ineffectual to reassure them. Marko was the right person for understanding the problem and the process for change. And now he was gone.

S am was pleased. His letter to Carla must have been okay because she called and offered him a job. After their phone conversation, he decided he would try and locate his father and tell him the good news.

Alan was on his way to St. Botolph Street when Sam called. He was happy with the opportunity to take a break from the case and invited him to have lunch at a little restaurant popular in this neighborhood. They would meet in an hour.

Sam arrived early since he wasn't sure about the location of this restaurant and decided he would spend some time looking around. He noticed a young woman about his age walking down the street towards him. She was tall, wearing a casual print short sleeve dress and low-heel sandals. Her dark hair was pulled up in a messy ponytail and she was clutching her bag close to her side as she walked. Sam decided to stop and ask her for directions to the restaurant.

"Excuse me, do you live around here?" Sam asked.

"What?" Maryanne asked apprehensively. She hadn't been feeling well that morning and asked her boss if she could leave work at noon. Still upset about Marko and the fire, she needed some time to think about her feelings about living in the city or moving to a smaller town.

"I'm sorry to disturb you, but I can't find the Botolph

Street Café."

"Oh, yes. It's just through the alley across the street."
A lot of people didn't know that the café was hidden in the
alley, and Maryanne was glad to help. As she started to unlock
the door to her building, Sam asked her another question. "I
wonder if you know of any apartments for rent around here?"

Maryanne looked at Sam carefully, trying to decide if
he was being truthful. But before she answered him, Sam
quickly said, "I'm Sam Sharp and my father is the detective
who's handling the fire investigation down the block. I'm
meeting him for lunch. I really am a good guy." He smiled and
could see Maryanne relax her shoulders and let out a deep
breath.

"It's just been so frightening lately. Does your father
know why the building caught on fire?"

Sam hadn't discussed this case with his father and, in
fact, had only read about it online. Now that he was going to
work at the center with Carla, maybe he should know more
about the facts and why Marko Miller had been killed. Sam
had read that Marko was a well-respected teen counselor.
People who worked with him must be shocked and upset.

"I don't really know much. But why don't I meet you
for coffee after lunch and I can tell you what I do know. There
has to be a Starbuck's around here." Once again Maryanne
hesitated. Did she really want to know more? However,
meeting with this guy might help her to sort out some of her
worries and doubts about the dangers in the city. After all, he
was the detective's son.

"Okay," Maryanne agreed, "there's a coffee shop at

the Copley Plaza. Let's meet there around 2:00." She then entered her building, realizing she hadn't even given Sam her name. Maryanne opened the door to her studio and sat on the sofa. It seemed that life was getting even more complicated.

Alan spent the rest of the morning reviewing his interview notes, as well as those of the first uniformed officers on the scene and waiting for the autopsy report to come through. He was pleased that Sam had called and wanted to go to lunch. This might give them a chance to review their schedules and establish some expectations. The other thing that was on Alan's mind was how thin Sam appeared. He might be feeling a lot of pressure because of all the changes in his life right now, but Alan was concerned enough to worry. He knew Sam had faced a lot of challenges before, but he seemed nervous, and Alan already noticed he was sleeping a lot. Maybe he should talk with Sam about this.

At 12:30 he walked into the small café on St. Botolph St. and saw that Sam already had a table.

"Hey, Dad!" Sam called out, "I have some good news!"

Alan seated himself at the round table and waited to hear what Sam was so excited about. "I got a job with Carla!" Sam smiled. "Lunch is on me. Thanks for your help getting a chance to meet with her."

Relieved and proud of his son, Alan asked the typical questions about salary, hours, commitment, and job descriptions. He would remember to thank Carla later. With this thought in mind, Alan decided it may be an opportune time to discuss part of the case with Sam, since he would undoubtably be hearing about Marko at work.

"As I briefly mentioned to you," Alan began, "I've been working the investigation of a recent house fire with a death involved. Knowing that you probably read about this online, I won't go into much detail. But the person who died worked with Carla at the center. His name was Markus Miller, but everyone called him Marko. He and I also worked together over the years on investigations involving teenagers and drugs. We became very good friends."

"I'm so sorry," Sam said. "You must feel awful, having to investigate the death of someone you personally knew. What happened? Did he live there? How come he didn't make it out?"

"Well," Alan said, "That's what I'm trying to find out. But, no, he didn't live there. I'm investigating what he was doing there and how the fire started."

Alan decided to change the subject away from the case. "I want you to know that my hours will be ragged for a while and so don't plan on me having regular dinners at home. Now that you'll be busy, too, maybe we can arrange our schedules for being home and taking care of Harry."

"If you want," Sam replied, "I can make a sort of calendar for us. It always worked with my roommates, so we didn't worry too much about each other. I can even show you how to put it on your phone."

"Great idea!" Alan was pleased with this idea and happy to know that Sam wanted to continue to stay with him.

He wondered if he even had a calendar on his phone as he plowed into his Club Sandwich.

As Sam devoured his roast beef sandwich, Alan considered if his fear about Sam's health was wrong. Maybe the security of a job and not worrying about a place to stay will get him on a better schedule of sleep and meals. However, Alan still planned to keep an eye out for signs of exhaustion or anxiety.

After lunch, Sam walked the few blocks to Copley Place to meet the girl, whose name he realized he didn't know. As he entered the high-end luxury building, he was impressed with the elegant marble walls and benches along with the cascading waterfall that pooled to an open fountain. A directory listed over 50 stores and restaurants on two levels that appeared to stretch a city block. Sam stood in wonder of this amazing Boston landmark and then noticed to the right of the entrance a small café where he saw her waiting for him.

Sam strolled casually over and put out his hand, "I'm sorry, but I don't know your name," he apologized. Maryanne told him her name, shook his hand, and smiled. As he sat down at the small table, she immediately wanted to know what he found out about the fire. Sam quickly ordered a cup of coffee before he continued the conversation. He didn't want to give the impression that his father always confided in him about ongoing investigations.

"I'm not certain what you've heard," Sam began, "but my father says there may be a murder investigation. The guy who died was a friend of his and it seems suspicious that he was even near that building. My father's talking to people who live in the area today. I didn't mention you to him, by the way."

Maryanne was relieved. "I did meet your father on Tuesday, at least I think it was that day. He gave me his card. But since I just moved in a couple of months ago, I doubt I could be of any help. The owner of my building and the guy next door are off on vacation for two weeks, so they probably won't be of any help either."

"Do you feel safe living here?" Sam asked. "It seems like a dangerous area for someone single. Maybe I'm making assumptions, though." Sam saw the hesitation on Maryanne's face and thought he probably went too far. Once again, he was projecting his values and concerns onto another. He knew nothing about her.

Maryanne took a moment to respond. She wasn't certain she was ready or willing to share her anxieties with a person she just met. Who was this guy anyway? She didn't know the answer, but in a moment of vulnerability she decided Sam was safe enough to talk to. After all, he was the son of the detective.

"I'm in the process of getting a divorce," she slowly began. "I've only been living on the East Coast for a couple of years, and I plan to move back to Washington State next year when everything gets settled."

"How long were you married?" Sam asked, and then kicked himself for prying.

"Only a couple of years. But it was a disaster from the beginning. Now I'm finding out that having a bad marriage puts me at the outside of society's mainstream anyway.

Divorce still has a negative connotation. It's still failure. And there's lots of pressure to explain what happened and make plans for what's next. I'm never sure what to say."

"I'm sorry to hear about that." Sam looked earnestly at Maryanne, willing for her to continue, or not.

"On a positive note, this has forced me to become more independent. My job at Barclay's Bank is secure enough and pays my expenses. I'm trying to save what I can. I only have one more year of college and hope to complete it. I'm studying to be an art therapist."

Sam listened and felt a certain kinship to Maryanne. Was that it, or did he feel protective? He thought he heard a little desperation in her voice because as she spoke, and talked faster, it seemed to be with less conviction. Maybe it was her innocent expectations or blind hope that things would get better, but he felt he could at least help her navigate through what had happened on the street.

"If you give me your number, I'll keep you informed about the investigation. Sometimes knowing the facts helps you to worry less."

He asked if he could meet with her again, under the guise of keeping her up on the case. But if he was truthful, he really wanted to get to know her better.

Alan left the restaurant and stopped again to admire the old buildings along St. Botolph Street. He noticed how gracefully they aged as they stood substantially intact, reminiscent of the Victorian Era. Feeling the unpredictability of old age, he almost envied the steadiness of these gracious buildings. They would never be the object of pity, or stereotyped, which was a commonplace experience of today's aging population. He thought of Sam and wondered if he knew how lucky he was to be young and healthy. Time would tell.

Alan walked down the block to the damaged building. He knew that the fire fighters had battled the blaze for hours and he expected there was nothing much left. The rooms would be drenched by the flood of water from the fire hoses which probably left a soggy path of destruction.

Entering the blackened front door, Alan could smell the scorched wood and saw the heavy layer of soot everywhere. The gritty sound of broken glass on the floor followed him around from room to room. The stairs leading up to the second floor were chewed up by the fire and flames had eaten up the walls and blackened the beams that were exposed in several rooms. The small kitchens and bathrooms in the first-floor apartments were covered in old linoleum that had blistered and buckled. All the furniture in the rooms looked like charcoal lumps. Alan knew he wouldn't find a clue anywhere.

Looking at his watch, Alan realized he only had twenty minutes to get to the agreed upon café and meet with Bret Grisham. He sounded like a nice kid on the phone, but Alan guessed that most Starbuck employees had a practiced and likable good nature.

Bret was waiting outside the small café when Alan pulled up. He appeared to be a mixed-race guy who looked younger than his profile that listed him at nineteen. Bret was slight and wore slim jeans and a shirt that was LGBT oriented.

Alan noticed and liked the derby hat on his head. He smiled at Bret and invited him to order anything he would like. "I'll just have some water," Bret decided, "I get so much coffee at work."

Alan got right to the point. "When was the last time you saw Marko?"

"I work odd hours and so we didn't really have a specific time to meet. He would usually call me when he had some time, and we would arrange something. The last time was a week ago Sunday after my shift. Around five o'clock."

"And how did it go? Did you think that Marko was worried about anything, or did you make plans to meet again?"

"Marko was good. He was really happy about how much I was getting done because I'm almost at the end of my program. We've been meeting for over a year, and he thought things were going well. He already talked with my boss and AA sponsor." At this point Bret lowered his head, "I'm just bummed about Marko dying. He was a great guy. Do you know what happened?"

"We're still in the initial stages of our investigation. I need to ask you what you were doing this past Saturday night and early Sunday morning."

"I knew you would ask me. I worked the late shift on Saturday and helped close around 10:00. And then I met up with my girlfriend to go to one of those 11:00 movies. We got out around 1:30 I think. I drove her home and then I went home. You can ask her, if you want to check."

Alan realized that Bret must have been in trouble at

one time. He had carefully prepared answers, and Alan believed him. He would still check with his employer and girlfriend. Giving Bret his card, he watched him walk down the street. Alan hoped that Marko's death would not set these kids back in any way.

The squad room was busy as usual when Alan returned. The printer was going, phones ringing, file drawers slamming and on top of everything was the smell of old coffee, sweat and the heat of the day. Above all that, he heard bursts of laughter. That could only mean one thing, Detective Enrique Mendez was back on the job. He had been away for two weeks, taking his wife and kids to Belize to visit his large extended family. This was a yearly event and he loved to return with funny stories about his many brothers and sisters and their life in the little town where they grew up. At thirty-five, Enrique was adventuresome and had a contagious energy that drew others to him. Alan liked working with him and was always impressed with his laser-like focus with investigations, along with his shrewd logic. Enrique believed they could always get to the truth by tenaciously digging through the piles of material they collected, even if some of it sounded like speculation. Alan needed his abilities now.

Enrique greeted Alan with a hug. "How'ya doing, boss? I heard we caught a case while I was gone." Alan quickly stepped out of the embrace and escorted Enrique into his office so he could organize his mind away from the clatter. Taking a chair beside Alan's desk, Enrique took out his notebook and ballpoint pen.

"I'm glad you're back," Alan sighed and sat down on

his old chair, "you probably already heard that Marko Miller died. He was killed in a fire that we suspect as arson." Without waiting for a response, Alan picked up some paperwork on his desk and read from the autopsy report. "The pathologist reported there were no carbon granules deposited in his bronchial passages or lungs and no carbon monoxide in his blood or other tissues. Therefore, he was dead before the fire broke out. Additionally, the lab tests reveal no alcohol, drugs or poisons in his system. They tell me the cause of death was attributed to multiple skull fractures apparently caused by repeated blows with a blunt instrument. The wounds were estimated to be caused by an object four or five inches in width."

"Wow," Enrique sighed, "it sounds like murder and arson all right. How far did the fire spread?"

"It was contained in that building. I'll give you the arson report, but basically, a large amount of gasoline was found. There were blackened splash marks and liquid trails going through the rooms. The fire marshal had a sophisticated method of verifying the point of origin and the course the fire had taken as it burned."

"Any witnesses?"

"That's the interesting part. Because the building has so many part-time residents, we may have difficulty reaching them. I'm trying to get names and numbers sorted. There are ten apartments in the building and all the tenants appeared to have been gone that weekend because the owner had scheduled a company to fumigate the building. I guess there was a rat problem. But anyway, there's some evidence this building was being used to sell drugs to local kids. There have also been frequent noise complaints because of teen parties on most weekends. That's where Marko comes into the picture. He was working with some addicted teens who were known to hang out at this location. My inclination is that's where they were buying their drugs. So, we've got to set up some interviews with the tenants and local people to find out what they know."

"Do you want me look into the residents?" Enrique asked, willing to get started.

"I need to get the list from the owner, David Reagan. He's out of town until Monday. We'll start talking to the residents then."

Alan took a moment to clarify his notes on the case. He sat down in his creaky chair and laid out how far he had gotten with the interviews. First, he told Enrique about his visit to Carla at the teen center and her explanation of Marko's work with teens, as well as their various programs.

"Because teens are known to be unpredictable and make dangerous choices," Alan wanted to emphasize, "this might have something to do with Marko's death. Especially since he was seen talking with several teenagers around that building on numerous occasions."

"Who else did you interview this week?" Enrique wrote quickly in his notes.

Alan related his meeting with Sidney, both at his office and at Marko's condo. He also mentioned Lily and the package with the wallet inside. He told Enrique of the three visits he had made to St. Botolph St., and speaking with Trudy and Maryanne. He lightly mentioned how vulnerable he thought Maryanne appeared in contrast to Trudy's cold and abrupt appearance.

"There were two others—friends of Marco's—who walked into the station after they heard about the investigation," Alan smiled at this. "His friend Jerome is an interesting character," he hesitated for a moment, "he's a gay guy who was out drinking with Marko the night before he died. Marko worked part-time designing outfits for a local drag theater, the Dragonfly, if you can believe that. Jerome is one of the entertainers. You can re-interview him and get a formal statement. Marko also helped design dresses for a woman whose shop, The Mystic Lady, is in the area. Her name is Alicia Grant and she's a bit overbearing but seemed dedicated to Marko. She let me know she would 'keep in touch'." Enrique rolled his eyes at this. "Again, you can get a formal statement from her."

"Another thing we need to do is find out what company David Reagan hired for the extermination. I wonder who complained to the health department. It usually takes months to get something done, so maybe they hired a private company."

Enrique said he would investigate this too. Together, they made a list of people they needed to meet. Alan wanted to visit the man on the corner of St. Botolph St. who owned the grocery store and then interview Eddie Pearson, another teen on Carla's list. Enrique was going to see if he could get some additional names of Marko's friends from Jerome. Alan called Sarah in Tech Services to have her go through Marko's computer to find his contacts and anything else of importance. They both made phone calls to set up interviews in the morning.

When Alan left his office, he immediately drove to his appointment with Rose. She greeted him at the door and noticed from his tight smile he appeared stressed. Rose understood clients may be anxious when beginning a counseling session and so she let Alan rest a minute in a comfortable easy chair. Drawing in a long breath and holding it for a minute before releasing it, Alan said, "It's been a difficult couple of days."

"I can imagine, Detective. Your line of work must take a lot out of you both physically and emotionally."

Rose waited again and then explained, "Alan, when you're comfortable, I'm going to begin by asking you to give me an earnest reflection of your life, and in doing so, I want you to remember that there are many ways to tell your story. I can give you a simple structure that will help."

"I like the idea that it will be simple," Alan smiled.

"Good. Let's begin with your family. When you were young, can you recall two or three family events which have special significance for you."

"Well, let's see, my father was very important in my life. He was a kind and honest man. I was proud that he was a quite well-known architect." Alan paused and then started again, "One of my fond memories was when he would drive us, my mother, brother and me, around the city and show us the buildings he worked on." Alan blinked a few times and seemed to appreciate this memory.

"My mother was very pretty and quiet. She had a lot of friends and encouraged my brother and me to get involved with activities. We both played tennis throughout college. She was the primary parent at home because my dad often worked late hours, sometimes coming home after we were asleep." Alan stopped to consider what to say next.

Understanding his reluctance to continue, Rose asked, "Would you say that you had a typically normal or maybe uneventful growing up experience?"

"Compared to others, I would say my early years were typical of a privileged family. Sometimes I was bored, but I was well taken care of and allowed to speak my opinion and was listened to. When I left for college, I believed that the world was going to be a much more interesting place than my neighborhood."

"Sometimes people are bored because of a recurring sense of inadequacy. Did you experience this at all?"

"I remember pushing away from my parents in my teens and falling short of their expectations." Alan thought for a moment, "Just like kids today, I guess. And because of this there were several times when I was probably filled with self-judgement."

"In what way?"

Alan sat back in his chair and cleared his throat. "Well, to begin with, there were always underlying values in my parent's rules and beliefs that I never really understood." Alan moved uncomfortably in his chair before continuing. "I remember one time, I was about nineteen I guess, and I overheard my parents talking about me. They were complaining that I wasn't 'doing' anything with my life, that I didn't have a set of goals to work towards. I felt angry and guilty for eavesdropping, but I was also scared they may be right."

"Did you confront them?"

"No, but I thought about it for years." Alan kneaded his hands together and tightened his lips. Confronting his parents was never on the books.

Rose knew talking about negative experiences helped, but she didn't want to push too hard. "Alan, this is a good example of a process of reflection. Reflection is looking back at something significant that happened and trying to make some sense of this experience. It sounds like this conflicting moment has stayed with you. Do you agree?"

"I guess it has. But I hadn't actually thought about it until now."

"To put it another way, we all inherit a story such as this from our upbringing, and in a small way, we might carry it with us and, sometimes, even let it define us."

Alan looked confused and needed more from this definition. "So, you're saying that I have been programmed to sometimes react, or make the choices I do, in response to my upbringing or expectations I carried with me. Is that right?"

"Perhaps. But the intention is not to identify causation, but to learn about ourselves. You might see your reflection in a specific experience such as you recalled, and it could generate emotion and uncertainty, but you're willing now to open up to a new way of looking at things."

Rose paused for a minute and then decided to take another approach. "Let's move on for a minute, Alan, did your parents have a good relationship?"

"As far as I know. My father always said the best thing that ever happened to him was being married to my mother. They didn't argue, as far as I noticed. But they were rather distant emotionally. We were not a family who hugged or expressed affection."

"Do you consider yourself to be an affectionate person?"

"Not really. Maybe this is because of how I grew up, but I know for a fact that both my wives complained about lack of emotion. I just don't feel comfortable with affection."

"Do you ever cry, Alan?"

Surprised by this question, Alan was beginning to feel defensive with his responses. "I've cried. When my father died, I cried. But it's not something I do to express emotion or to relieve feelings of sorrow. Although, I must admit this week I was struggling with my emotions after I learned that my friend had died. Maybe it was anger, but I was certainly distraught."

Rose thought for a moment and then explained, "Communicating anger, or any emotion, shows you're willing to share thoughts and experiences and then see what insights might emerge."

"Well," Alan admitted, "I suppose I always build a wall around my world, probably to hide some pain or some unfulfilled goal."

"Can you tell me one unfulfilled goal you have?"

Alan squirmed in his chair, hoping their time would end soon, and he didn't have to deal with his past or his growing discomfort. "I'm not sure how to answer that. Maybe it's my need for companionship. Right now, I seem to be drifting through my maze of work and wishing I had a companion or friend to talk things over with."

"Very insightful, Alan. This is a good place to start. Learning to listen to your inner voice may be the first step to understanding your conflicts and responsibilities. We can focus on your desire for relationships as we move ahead."

When the fifty-minute session was over, Alan wondered if therapy was going to work. How much of him could ever be fixed? To even ask sounded cynical. Maybe focusing on a longer goal, like relationships, would offer some enlightenment and calm his fears and pessimism. He'd have to think about it.

# FRIDAY, MAY 20<sup>TH</sup>

Tony expected to hear from the police sooner or later, so he wasn't surprised to see Detective Sharp waiting for him when he opened the store first thing in the morning. He invited Alan inside and locked the door behind him. He didn't want anyone to interfere with the conversation. He pointed to a small café table and asked Alan to have a seat.

Tony was always a bit apprehensive about giving anyone, especially the police, the impression that he was connected to the local comings and goings of the neighborhood. Always a keen observer, he couldn't help but be aware of who was doing what with whom on the surrounding streets, but his loyalty and common sense made him protective of his neighbor's privacy. After owning his store for over twenty-five years, he knew a lot about the history of the neighborhood and the people who lived there. Over the years he enjoyed the improvements and growing community spirit, but he was still aware of the criminal element hiding behind the street's exterior.

"How can I help you, detective?"

"Did you know Marko Miller?" Alan smiled slightly at the older man, hoping to gain his confidence and learn about his connection with the neighborhood.

"Yes, I did know Marko. And I liked him, he was a good guy, trying his best to turn kids' lives around. I am just sick to know he's dead." Tony glanced away and shook his head. "Why do all the good guys have to die?"

Alan nodded in agreement and then kept to his script, "What do you know about the house that was targeted? There's word on the street it was a drug house. Do you agree?"

"I've heard rumors for years. There's been a lot of activity around that place, especially on the weekends. Criminals, drug dealers, people strung out, noises at all hours, and teens who have nothing else to do but get high. They all know that's the place to find whatever they needed." As Tony talked, he began making coffee in the self-serve coffee machine perched on a near-by counter. He measured out the coffee grains and said, "I've called the police numerous times, but nothing has ever been done. We've tried a block watch, but owners are worried about getting involved. There is this one lady, Trudy, who called Marko a lot because the police didn't help. She's a nuisance, but at least she tries." Tony sounded exasperated.

"Can you give me any information on the people who live at that address? We're attempting to speak with them, but we understand no one was home at the time of the fire."

"People come and go all the time. There are a few regular renters, but it's had the reputation of being a flop house over the years. I'm surprised one of the wealthy owners on the block didn't try to purchase it. Do you know who owns it?"

"We're tracking that down. It appears to be owned by a real estate company. It seems a little shady if they let it go downhill over the years. When was the last time you saw Marko?"

Setting a steaming mug of coffee on the table for Alan, Tony tilted his head and stared into the distance as he recalled, "I guess it was on Friday afternoon, a week ago. He wanted to know if I would keep an eye on one of his kids. He worried the kid was getting involved with drugs again after he was seen on the block, hanging around that building. I liked to help Marko out like this. He was devoted to the programs at the Teen Center and wanted to make sure the kids knew the importance of staying clean and beginning a new life. Gosh, it's hard to believe he's dead." Once again, Tony looked away and shook his head.

"Who was the kid Marko wanted you to watch?"

"Eddie something, he's the one who wears the weird clothes. You really can't miss him."

Understanding Tony's genuine affection for Marko, Alan asked him what he really wanted to know. "Do you have any idea who would want Marko dead?"

Tony shook his head, "No! Like I said, he was a good guy."

The men continued to talk about the neighborhood and the growing concern about drugs. Tony reminisced about the history of the street and the change that has occurred. Alan thanked Tony for his dedication to his customers and the community and asked him to call if he thought of any concerns or remembered anything else that might help the investigation.

Tony walked Alan to the door and then remembered, "Oh, Detective, the Block Watch captain, Ron, said he was keeping a list of unfamiliar vehicles that drive through the street. Do you want his number?"

Alan wrote down the number and waved as he left the store.

The next meeting Alan had scheduled was with the Keaton Insurance Company which covered the burned building. Its enviable location was across from the Boston Common, the 50-acre park which was the oldest municipal park in the country. The office resided in the Financial District, near the cobblestone streets of Beacon Hill, drawing most of their business from those who could afford the steep rents, both personal and professional. Alan was impressed and somewhat intimidated by the luxury.

As he entered the building through the leaded glass doors, Alan was met by a receptionist who appeared ready to help. The insurance company was located on the 20th floor, and he was pointed to the elevators. Another receptionist met him as the elevator door opened and asked if he had an appointment. Alan noted the inlaid marble floors and tall ceilings along with the oak paneling on the walls. Once again, he marveled at the wealth lawyers, brokers and other professionals surrounded themselves in. He pulled out his ID and told the very young woman he was here to talk with Les Quinn.

"Can I tell him what this is about?" she coldly asked.

Somewhat irritated, Alan firmly stated, "I have an appointment with Mr. Quinn. Tell him I'm inquiring about the building on St. Botolph Street and the fire last Sunday."

As Alan waited, he reviewed his conversation with Tony. He was certainly upset about Marko's death, but he seemed to be protecting his business or his customers. Maybe Alan was overreacting to their conversation, as he sometimes did when he lost a lead or found himself in a corner. But if Tony could influence some of the residents of that building to speak up about the drug business on the block, he knew it might help identify the sellers and protect the neighborhood from additional harm. Alan sighed, Marko would have instinctively known how to get the residents' trust and cooperation.

Looking at his watch, Alan realized with irritation that he had been sitting there for thirty minutes. When he was finally escorted into Quinn's office, Alan let the man know he didn't appreciate having to wait and reminded him this was a homicide investigation. He expected cooperation. The insurance man looked unconcerned and offered Alan a plain wood chair by his desk.

Quinn's office was clutter-free with a surprisingly unsophisticated air. The large desk was dark wood and so plain that it looked like an ad for less is more. The only color in the room was the abstract painting in monochromatic tones that hung over a black sofa and matching chairs. The man himself wore a plain grey suit, black tie, and white shirt. He was starting to bald, and Alan noticed a tired expression of distain on his face.

Alan got right to the point. "Our research shows the building on St. Botolph Street that burned is owned by David Reagan. Is that right?"

"Yes," Quinn responded, "but I don't legally represent him. I just take care of all the insurance matters and his legal team is another firm. How can I help you?"

"How much was the building insured for?"

Quinn hesitated and then pulled out a file to check on the numbers. "It was insured ten years ago for $4,000,000. At the time, Reagan was the new owner and expected the equity to increase dramatically over the years, especially with the improvements being made to the area."

"That seems to be very high coverage, especially since I understand he made few improvements on this building. Was he aware of the reputation this building had?"

"You would have to check with him or his legal team about that. We've sent our adjusters to examine the damage and are waiting for the official police report before we make any final decisions. Do you have an idea when the report will get to us?"

Alan was not willing to give any information on the investigation, especially given that Quinn remained so formal with his answers. "Do you know which exterminating company was used for the problems the building was having?"

"No," Quinn frowned, "that's not my business."

Alan asked a few more questions and then left his card. Hopefully, he would get more answers from David Reagan, the owner of the building.

As long as he was in the city, Alan decided to walk over to Faneuil Hall for lunch. Maybe he would see if Sidney Miller would like to join him. He had promised to keep him advised on how the investigation was going.

It was a beautiful spring day. A breeze had sprung up and white fluffy cumulus clouds promenaded across the blue sky. People walking by seemed as enchanted with the day as Alan. He noticed older men and women walking arm and arm with no destination but to find somewhere they might pass the hours. Alan, feeling a slight tinge of jealousy, considered what he might do in later years, and then quickly dismissed the thought.

On the way to Sidney's office, he passed by Barclay's International Bank and remembered it was where Maryanne, the young girl he met earlier, worked. He made a mental note to speak with her again at some point. She seemed anxious about the fire and police activity, and he still felt a little protective of her. He wondered what she was doing the night of the fire.

Sidney Miller had just returned from court and was thinking about lunch. He was surprised when he heard that Detective Sharp was waiting to talk with him.

"How can I help you, Detective? I'm just on my way to lunch." Sidney said.

"Can I join you?" Alan asked. "I'm starving and only have a limited time. Maybe we can go to Ari's BBQ in the Market if you don't have a preference." Both men agreed on this popular restaurant.

Faneuil Hall Marketplace was the center of tourist attractions in the city. It offered an eclectic mix of shopping options along with top rated restaurants and a world-famous Food Colonnade. One of the oldest established eateries was Ari's BBQ which was started in 1976. If you got there early enough, you might beat the crowd of hungry tourists who stood for hours in line to get the slow cooked brisket. Today being Friday, the line was long, but seemed to be moving quickly.

As they waited, Alan asked Sidney how long he had lived in Boston. "Oh, let's see, about fifteen years, I guess. I started out in a law firm closer to home in Chicago. But the crime was so prevalent and dangerous, that I decided to spend my final years of law in a better environment. Although, I wonder now if that's the case. I love Boston, but I'm getting tired of the corruption in every large city."

"Do you have family living with you?" Alan knew he was prying, but he really was beginning to like this man.

"No, I never married," Sidney replied. "I thought about it, of course, and seemed to have opportunities along the way, but I was married to my job. Now, of course, I wish it could be different. Maybe I would be a grandfather by now!"

Alan drew in a breath and confessed, "I have two grown kids and two grandchildren who I never see because they live on the West Coast. After two marriages, I'm single too. You never know how life's going to turn out. I've gotten used to being on my own, but now my son has moved in! He says it's just until he can find something else, but we know how that goes."

"Do you get along with your son?" Sidney inquired.

"I do, although we have very different personalities. He wants to save the world and I want to fight crime. In fact, he just got hired at the teen center by Carla. He's going to do some research and grant writing for her."

"She's a nice woman," Sidney commented, "I got the impression she liked Marko and valued the work he did with the teens. Funny, I just didn't see him in that kind of work. He always seemed so flighty and caught up in his colorful friends."

Ordering their meals, the two men found a table away from most of the crowd so they could talk freely. Alan once again thought how different the two brothers were. Marko's personality was upbeat and outgoing, whereas Sidney seemed to be more reflective and practical in Alan's opinion. On the other hand, they both appeared to share a confidence and ability to make good decisions. Alan appreciated both men.

"When was the last time you spoke with Marko?"

"I tried to get ahold of him just before the holidays. I left a message on his phone, or at least the last number I had for him. I never knew if he got the message or not. So, I guess the last time I really saw him was when I met you and Marko at that café. He didn't seem to want much conversation, and, truthfully, neither did I. Of course, now I regret being so arrogant. He was my brother, and I should have tried harder to understand him. Now I find out that he's been doing such wonderful work with teens, and I would have supported him any way I possibly could. It saddens me to know I'll never get the chance to tell him how proud I am of him."

"We all have regrets, Sidney. Sometimes I think it's just the inescapable and insistent fact of being the age we now are. In fact, it often seems that whatever we value most is finally taken away. Children, loved ones, opportunities for adventure and even some physical abilities seem to fade out of our grasp." Alan smiled and looked tentatively at his companion. "If we were wise about these things, we probably should learn how to let go and move on." Alan took a long sip of his coke and thought he was beginning to sound like Rose.

"So, when did you become the philosopher, detective?" Sidney laughed. "Tell me, how is the investigation going so far?"

Alan was glad to get back to talking about business. "I've interviewed a number of people who knew Marko and I've several more to talk to. I wish I could say there's been significant progress, but we're really at the initial phase of the investigation."

"Please let me know what you find out. My family is concerned, and as you can imagine, we're grieving for our brother."

They both finished their lunches and promised to meet again when more news about Marko became available. Alan understood that if Sidney didn't have any contact with his brother, he wouldn't know anything about Marko's schedule on the days before his death.

As Alan walked away, he thought about his own brother and made a mental note to call him soon. He felt a pang of remorse for not keeping in touch. Alan always used his job as an excuse, even though he knew he was only kidding himself. On the other hand, why didn't his brother call him? He wondered if family relationships mirrored each other. Maybe loneliness was universal. He shook his head and let this thought drift away.

Eddie Pearson was anxious about meeting with the detective. Marko had been his only champion and Eddie was frightened by what the police wanted to know. He was even more worried about the dealer who was after him. He didn't feel safe. The fight-flight-freeze reflex had really kicked in since Saturday night. Eddie thought about putting up a brave front and facing his drug dealer, but he knew it would only be putting himself in more danger. Not a good idea. He could run, leave the city, but where would he go? He even thought of fabricating a lie and trying to pin what he knew on someone else. But mostly he hoped he would be given more time. His fear and anxiety were triggered, and he was losing the ability to process the situation. His heartbeat pulsated in his head.

Alan waited patiently and watched Eddie walk down the school hall to the conference room. He was almost six feet tall with spikey greased bleached hair. Dressed in black and obviously wearing eye liner, he looked older than the other students. His swagger and the stomping of his heavy boots revealed an attitude that Alan was not looking forward to. Holding out his hand, he shook Eddie's limp fingers and escorted him into a conference room. He got right to the point.

"When was the last time you saw Marko Miller."

"I dunno," Eddie mumbled.

"Okay, we can do this interview here or we can go to the station. I have your father's number and he can meet us there." Alan was not going to play games with this kid. He didn't really need to have his father present because Eddie was over 18. But since he was still in high school, he thought Eddie might want some support.

"I saw him for my appointment. It was maybe Wednesday, that's when we usually meet." Eddie stared angrily at Alan. "Why don't you just ask the people at that center, they have my schedule somewhere."

"Where were you on Saturday and Sunday early morning last weekend?" Alan kept his eyes fixed on Eddie. He wasn't sure he trusted this kid. He had done some quick research on Eddie's background and knew he was from a very affluent family. His father was a stockbroker and his mother worked in finance.

Eddie slapped a hand on his knee in obvious frustration. "I don't know where I was! Just hanging around with my friends. That's all we ever do on the weekends."

"Can I have a list of their names to confirm your story? I need to know if you were anywhere near St. Botolph Street on either day." Alan got out a pencil and paper for Eddie to write on. He noticed a little panic in the kid's eyes. Maybe he wasn't as tough as he thought, or maybe he had some information he didn't want Alan to know.

"Do I need a lawyer?" Eddie asked belligerently. Surprised, Alan told him this was not a suspect interview, and he was free to go anytime. If he helped now, he might be eliminated from the list of people they were interviewing. Eddie stood up and left the room.

Well, thought Alan. That was interesting. He decided to call Carla and find out more about Eddie before he continued to question him.

Enrique spent the morning talking with a computer tech at the precinct. So far, all he'd found on Marko's laptop were the usual emails and searches which were related to both of his jobs. Because Marko designed several of the trans and drag queen's glamourous gowns, there appeared to be several sites from well-known designers. It seemed like Marko had a knack for following popular singers and actors online and knocking off their dresses. It was like looking at 'before' and 'after' photos people generally enjoyed. Enrique noticed a photo of Celine Dion in a low-slung sequined gown and next to it the same gown, in a much larger size, on one of the drag entertainers. Marko had been very talented.

The other searches and emails were connected to his job at the teen center. He had lists of rehab programs, AA and NA meeting places, transitional housing, food banks and other sites that could be of help to addicts, or kids down on their luck. Marko also had names and numbers for counselors who offered their services pro-bono or on a sliding scale. Enrique knew this was typical information collected when working with people who needed help.

The only perplexing item on Marko's computer was a folder marked "Details." It had three pages full of initials and numbers. The numbers could be dates and times and the initials could be the teens he worked with. Enrique made a copy of the pages and put it in the folder he kept on the investigation.

He had three appointments scheduled for the day. His first stop was with Jerome at his workplace, a drag club twenty minutes away. Enrique wanted to learn more about the time he and Marko had spent together the night before his death. He also planned to talk with Lily and learn more about Marko's personal life. He and Alan were still trying to track down Marko's movements on that Saturday. Enrique's final appointment led him to St. Botolph Street.

Jerome loved Marko like a brother. He remembered the day they met when Marko was working at the music store and learned Jerome was an entertainer. He had been thrilled when Marko accepted his invitation to drop by and watch a show. It surprised them both when the drag queen world rose like a beacon for Marko and his design talents. Jerome remembered how happy he was to leave the music store job and immediately begin designing styles for drag costumes. He was gifted and understood there was an art to making the male form look feminine. It involved big hips, big boobs, and big hair. The goal was to look like a real woman. There was a lot of math involved, especially when you needed to prepare the gowns for all the movements the queen might do. Every job was a challenge and Marco loved it.

Jerome mourned his friend and readily agreed to meet the other detective on the case at the theater. But when he entered Marko's studio area, Jerome was hit with a grief so tangible it hurt his whole being. He had been in shock when he first heard that Marko was dead. He then went from feeling numb, to being in acute pain. Looking around now at the fabrics and sewing equipment that his friend so lovingly cared for, he felt an overwhelming surge of loneliness. This aloneness was an ache that he thought would never leave his heart. He was determined to feel this pain and the reality of loss rather than go into denial like a lot of people tried to do. He hoped by recognizing Marko's death and trying to help with the investigation, he would be honoring his friend.

Jerome could not make sense of anybody wanting to kill Marko. As he thought about it, his anger built. He wanted to blame someone and see that they were punished. Rifling through Marko's top drawer of threads and needles, Jerome came across a key. The tag attached to the keychain was simply labeled with a number. Maybe this was his mailbox key, Jerome first thought, but then remembered those keys were smaller. Did Marko have a security box at the bank? Or a post office box somewhere? At any rate, he needed to give the key to the detective. Keys sometimes solved crimes. He continued his search for clues.

Enrique arrived at the Dragonfly on time to meet with Jerome. He was surprised to see how ordinary the outside of the theater appeared. White-washed brick, with several glass windows holding posters of upcoming shows, the building appeared like any theater around town. The front entrance was unlocked and so Enrique stepped into the lobby. It was carpeted in a bright purple rug scattered with tiny yellow stars. Stairs leading up to the balcony were on both sides of the room and there appeared to be a bar set up for drinks and food purchases. Looking around for Jerome, Enrique wondered if he should call out or find his way to the dressing rooms. Before he could decide, Jerome made his entrance.

Dressed in a red caftan and pointy black shoes with one-inch heels, Jerome held out his arms to Enrique for a brief hug. "I'm so glad you're here. I'm having such a sad day because I cry every time I think of poor Marko." Jerome swept his fingers under his eyes to keep his mascara from running. "Come on back to the dressing area where we can talk in Marco's studio for privacy." Walking expertly on his heels, Jerome led the way with a little sway of the glossy material he wore. Enrique smiled and followed.

The room was smaller than expected. Taking over one side wall were two racks of glamourous dresses hanging wildly on hangers. They seemed to compete for attention because of the adornments of sequins and beads and ruffles. Mirrors dominated another wall with a long counter running under them. Makeup, wigs, and anything the men needed to look like women were scattered all around. Jerome invited Enrique to sit on one of the folding chairs next to counter.

"How can I help?" Jerome pleaded. "I want to do anything I can to help you find Marko's killer." Enrique thought for moment and then, taking out his note pad and pen asked his first question. "Was Marko seeing anyone?"

"No! Marko wasn't seeing anyone. And I would know if he was because I was always trying to set him up with dates. He said he wasn't interested. I always wondered if maybe he had been hurt at some time and the rejection was just too much." Jerome fiddled with a makeup brush on the counter as he spoke. "You know, I thought he was gay, but I can't even be certain about that!" His eyebrows, which were evenly sculpted, were raised in question.

Enrique inquired about clubs or gyms or anything that Marko may have been involved with. Jerome just shook his head. 'What kind of friends were these?' Enrique thought. If they got together for dinners, they must have wondered about Marko's relationships. He was going to have to dig deeper.

"Detective Sharp said that you and Marko had drinks and dinner at the Ritz on that Friday. Can you think of anything he said that might have worried him?"

Jerome shook his head back and forth. "I told him we were only there to celebrate that night. His gowns at the show were a huge success and I insisted that our conversation revolve around his talent. Marko was a humble guy and I wanted to let him know how proud we all were of him."

"When you left him that night, how did you know he got home safely?"

"I ordered a personal Uber. Marko was in no shape to get himself home safely. I'm afraid we ordered too much to drink and not enough sustenance. Anyway, the Uber driver is a friend of mine and I called him later. He said that he walked Marko to the door and watched him get in the elevator."

"So, you didn't hear from Marko the next day?"

"I left him a voicemail, but I knew he had a big meeting all morning. I wish I would have called him again." Jerome started to tear up and grabbed for a Kleenex.

"How about Marko's clients? Was anyone upset with him or demanding or have any reason at all to hurt him?"

"No! I promise you this detective. We all loved him! Who would ever want to hurt such a generous, kind guy like Marko?"

Enrique asked for the name of the Uber driver and decided to end the conversation. "Jerome, you were obviously very close to Marko. I want you to keep thinking about Marko's personal life especially and call me if anything occurs to you." Enrique stood up, accidentally bumping into a mannequin he hadn't noticed beside the door. Jerome looked as if he were going to hug again, and so Enrique quickly turned and walked away.

Jerome felt for the key in his pocket. Why didn't he give it to the detective?

Enrique's next stop was to meet with Lily, Marko's neighbor. She seemed very agreeable on the phone and invited him to meet at her condo. When he knocked on her door, she insisted on seeing his badge and credentials before unhooking the chain on the door. Once approved, she welcomed him in. Her small place was charming, although somewhat eccentric. She seemed to prefer pastel colors that offset the lavender walls. The prints on the walls were flower scenes similar to the lovely renaissance impressionist's art of the eighteenth century. Books were scattered everywhere giving the impression that she was reading several novels at once. Enrique also noticed a Persian cat, lounging lazily on a beautiful handmade quilt of multiple intricate colors and designs. Lily smiled and directed him to the overstuffed chair by the window. When she offered coffee or tea, he declined.

"Thank you for talking with me today, Lily. Detective Sharp informed me about the package you delivered to Marko's condo. It had his wallet inside, and you said you didn't know who sent it." Enrique was reading from the notes he had written about the case so far. "How often do packages come for Marko?"

"I don't know exactly because I usually only get them when Marko's away. He buys all those statues and when they're being sent, he wants to be certain they're safe. I'm almost always home, so I don't mind taking them for him." Lily sat on the sofa next to her cat and stared intently at Enrique, determined to give accurate information.

"I understand that Marko has occasional parties for friends. Are you usually invited?" Lily nodded. "Can you give me the names of his friends?"

For the first time, Lily hesitated. "I'm not comfortable giving out names. It seems like a privacy issue, doesn't it?"

"I understand your concern," Enrique began, "but we're gathering as much information as we can to find out what happened to your friend. Let me ask you about a few people he may have known. I've already spoken to Jerome, so how about Teddy, Stuart, Michael, and Robert? Do these names sound familiar?

"Yes. I know all of them. They were the guys from the club and were always invited to Marko's parties. Everyone would bring a dish and wine or beer and talk and laugh all night long." Lily blushed and admitted, "They were real gossips. I loved all the stories they told."

"When was the last time you were all together?"

"The week before last. Marko had just bought a new statue, a black cat that looked Egyptian, and he wanted to celebrate. He always had a party when he bought a new animal." Lily teared up when she said this. Obviously, she was going to miss her friend.

"Was there ever a disagreement or misunderstanding between any of them? Perhaps a discussion that got out of control?"

"No. They did yell and carry on, but it was always in good fun. I think they were all into drama, especially since they were entertainers. One thing though, they always wanted Marko to quit his job at the teen center and work full time with them. He would laugh and refuse, but they just kept at him."

"My last question, Lily, is where were you on Saturday night?"

"Here, with my cat. I was watching "Scandal." Lily looked apologetic.

Enrique nodded and thanked Lily as he handed her his card. He asked her to call if any more packages were delivered or if she thought of anything else that would help the case. His next stop was to meet Trudy on St. Botolph Street.

Trudy was irritated by having to speak with another detective. The more she stayed away from the investigation, the safer she was. All she needed to know was when an official police report would be written that guaranteed her remodeling work could begin. She was desperate to sell and get out of the neighborhood. When Enrique arrived, she brusquely allowed him into her building. Once seated, Trudy asked in a crisp manner, "What is it that you want now?"

"Thank you for taking the time to speak with me," Enrique noticed Trudy's abrasiveness and continued, "we're still wondering where you were on the night of the fire. My notes say you brought your child to a neighbor's place when you realized the danger. What happened exactly to make you aware of the fire?" Enrique was getting annoyed with the sullen look Trudy gave him.

Trudy took a long breath of exasperation and lied, "I could smell the smoke coming from next door! Obviously, there was a fire! It was early in the morning, and I could even hear crackling or knocking of some sort that sounded odd. What do you think I would do? I had my child with me!" She hoped he wouldn't press her anymore about that night. If anyone knew that she had left her daughter alone, she would be in serious trouble.

"Where is your child now?" Enrique was losing patience.

"She lives with her father. I see her on weekends if they don't have plans. Right now, they live in upstate New York and it's not always easy for me to travel there. Why is that so important?"

"We're just trying to establish details. Who was the neighbor you left your daughter with?"

Trudy squirmed. "Her first name is Maryanne. She lives a few doors down. I'm really not good with last names."

Enrique raised his eyebrows enough to question this statement. Trudy stared back at him.

"Did you know Marko Miller? The man who died that morning?"

"I only knew him because I heard he worked at the Roxbury teen center. Some of the neighbors saw him talking to several of the kids who were hanging around that building. So when I called the teen center to see if they could do anything about the noisy kids, they had me talk to him. I had hoped he would get them out of our neighborhood." Trudy let out a sigh of disgust. "I'd called the police a couple of times about the noise that blared from that building at all hours, but they did nothing."

Enrique noticed she was getting upset by these questions, but decided to ignore her obvious displeasure and continue, "We have a witness who said they saw you talking with Marko last week. It looked like the conversation was heated. Do you remember this?"

"Who said that?" Trudy was nervous now and quickly tried to recall when this had happened. "I guess I did speak with him when I saw him walking down the street one day. I expected him to help me, but he seemed amused by my concerns. He told me to call the police. I might have been a little mad at some point because I had called the police and like I said, you guys did nothing!" Trudy worried that being caught in a lie was making her more dramatic than necessary.

"Let's go back to the night of the fire. After you dropped off your daughter, what did you do next?"

"When I got back to my building, the firemen were already trying to douse the fire , and the police were telling people to disperse. I ran up to my condo to see if I should get things like my wallet, phone, and computer, you know, things that are important. And then I got in my car and drove around to another parking place, away from the fire. I sat in my car for a long time."

"Did you call anyone?"

"No. I was too upset."

"When did you pick up your daughter"

"Maybe around 5:30. It was just getting light out."

"Do you have any idea who would have set the fire? Or anyone who wanted to harm Marko Miller?"

"Of course not!"

"If you hear anything, please let us know." Enrique handed his card to Trudy. He stood up and was relieved to walk away from this obnoxious woman. The neighborhood will be much improved when she moves out, he thought.

As Enrique was leaving Trudy's building, he was stopped abruptly by a man with a clipboard. "Excuse me, are you one of the detectives investigating the fire?"

Enrique looked at the short, determined man who seemed to be breathing heavily. "Yes, I am."

"I'm the Block Watch captain for the street and I have some information that may help with the investigation."

"Okay," Enrique was trying not to roll his eyes, just in

case the nervous man did have something that would give him leads.

"I have a list of cars, trucks and vans that regularly travel on this street. When they're not familiar to me, I jot down the license plate, car color, and make."

"Do you have the list dated?"

"Of course," Ron looked a bit askance to think he would ever leave an important detail like that off a formal list. "Here are the lists for this month."

Enrique took the clipboard from Ron and scanned it. "Can I take this with me to make a copy?"

"I already made a copy for myself. It's valuable information at our monthly block meetings."

Enrique imagined how the other members probably responded to this officious man's offerings. He knew people like Ron, those who needed to feel important and helpful and had a peculiar way of interacting with others. To be respectful, he shook Ron's hand and thanked him.

"Detective," Ron raised his eyebrows, "You will get back to me and let me know how the investigation is going." Enrique just smiled.

Alan returned to the office with enough time to catch Carla on the phone before she left work. He recounted his conversations with the three teens he had interviewed, hoping that Carla would know more about them. But Carla had no personal insights because she didn't work with them directly.

"I trusted Marko to handle their cases and let me

know if he had problems. As far as I knew, things were going very well." Carla hesitated for a minute, "Eddie Pearson is a spoiled kid from a wealthy family, and I'm not surprised he walked away from you, Alan. He's been in rehab several times and it just doesn't stick. But I really don't believe that any of those three kids had anything but respect and friendship with Marko." She promised to keep her ears open for any negative comments or conversations.

When Enrique arrived back at the office, he gave Alan the list of vehicles Ron had handed him. This information may come in handy when they needed witnesses and so Alan added it to his file. He was ready to review the case with his partner.

"I feel as though we're up against the clock here for some reason. Maybe it's because the lieutenant wants results ASAP, and we have no leads." Alan tapped his pencil on the table, as if typing out an answer. "Usually, we look at the nearest relative, but this time the victim's nearest and dearest couldn't be responsible. Marko's family didn't even know where he lived. So, we'll have to look further afield. Somewhere in Marko's life he may have interacted with the killer in such a way as to provoke him or her to violence." Alan leaned over his desk and cleared his throat, "Let's assume that the murderer has found something out about Marko that is truly intolerable, so much so that he can no longer let him live."

"Or he was just at the wrong place when something was going down." Enrique suggested,

"But if that's the case, what was he doing at that

empty building so late at night?"

So far, they had interviewed the people who knew Marko well, and yet, they still didn't know his movements after Friday, his night out with Jerome. If he did go back to his condo that night, then they had to find out what he was doing all day Saturday.

"You're right about something," Enrique agreed. "Whatever event set this off and if it included Marko, it has to involve the arson. I think we need to put together a timeline for Marko, starting with Sunday morning and go backward minute by minute to see what placed him at the scene and, perhaps, set this into motion."

"How did your interviews go today?" Alan pulled out his notes to review, pushing aside the mess of paperwork that was accumulating.

"I sure don't like that lady Trudy," Enrique related. "She's cold as ice and completely uncaring about Marko. I wonder how she got so mean. When she told me that her daughter stayed with her ex, I was overjoyed for her daughter!" Enrique shook his head and thought about his own daughters who were jewels in his life.

"I agree," Alan responded, "You just wonder why some people have kids. Did you find out anything about her movements the night of the fire?"

"She took her daughter to a neighbor and then sat in her car. That's it. But she's lying about something, or maybe everything! I couldn't leave fast enough."

"How did it go with Jerome?"

"He was obviously a good friend of Marko's. Jerome

wanted Marko to quit the teen center and work full time as a designer. I guess he was terrific. As far as Jerome knew, Marko didn't have any problems or know of anyone who might be after him. He was just a great guy. And when I interviewed Lily, I got the same impression. Everyone loved Marko."

"So, we have to dig deeper. I spoke with the three teenagers, and they didn't seem suspicious. Although Eddie Pearson was questionable." Alan related the experience he had with the arrogant teen. "We just need to find out what Marko was doing last Saturday. I want you to go through his computer again and see if you can find a calendar or a list of places he might go. Did he belong to a gym? Did he take classes? Was he dating anyone? We still don't have a full picture of his personal life."

Alan continued, "I'll double check the information Carla gave me and then look into Marko's bank account and bills and whatever else pops up."

In the meantime, there were several questions that needed to be answered. Did the lists of numbers and dates on Marko's computer have any importance to his death? Was Marko keeping track of the teens and following them? Who were the dealers in this area? Were all the apartments really empty on that night?

"Did you get in touch with the Health Department about the complaints on the building?"

Enrique shook his head, "I left a message."

Alan was planning to speak with the vice cops on patrol in the St Botolph St. area to get a better idea of the activity on the street and any known drug dealers who sold there. He had yet to contact the owner of the burned building, David Reagan, because he was out of town until Monday. If he had to talk with Reagan's attorney, Alan considered asking Sidney to accompany him. Being family and a lawyer, Sidney might help get answers quicker. A second later, Alan realized this would probably be an apparent conflict of interest, so he decided against it.

Enrique mentioned the four friends who attended Marko's parties regularly. He would try to get in touch with them, too. Enrique and Alan decided to meet at the station again the following day around 1:00 for lunch to share any new information they found.

Sam completed his first day at the teen center which involved a lot of paperwork along with meeting several of the counselors on staff. They all talked about Marko and how much they missed him. The drug scene on St. Botolph Street was well known and everyone worried that the teens they worked with could easily find dealers around that building. Apparently, Marko had been zeroing in on a specific person he thought was dealing, but no one knew who it was.

Sam also overheard that many of the teens who were regulars at the center were severely addicted to drugs of various kinds. Many were in a downward spiral, unable to function, and in danger of homelessness, going to jail, or even mental impairment and death, unless they got treatment for their drug abuse, anxiety, and depression. They came to the center because it was one of the few resources available to them. It was safe and non-judgmental and offered them a real chance to turn their lives around. Although he would not be working personally with the teens, Sam felt a kinship with them because of his own problem with Adderall.

Now that he was starting a new job, Sam believed he needed the Adderall more than ever before. He took it by pill, not wanting to be caught with any paraphernalia associated with hard core drugs. He knew kids who snorted or shot up the drug, but he had drawn the line. The reason he took the drug, he told himself, was because it gave him more confidence, especially socially. He was never a shy person, but Sam knew he lacked the social skills many of his classmates seemed to possess naturally. Once he had enough Adderall in his system, he felt more on top of things, more self-assured and his brain seemed to function better and faster which helped him with his studies—and now with his job.

Sam was aware of how conflicting his use of Adderall was while working at the center, but he considered it a temporary aide. He would stop just as soon as he became comfortable with the new routines and demands of the job. He scanned some of the Center's pamphlets and noticed there were any number of AA and NA meetings in the Boston area. He had tried meetings before and didn't think they helped him. But he jotted down some addresses on his phone, just-in-case. Based on what he read about Adderall online, he knew he would have to undergo a period of detoxification if he chose to stop taking the pills. But clearly, this was not the right time.

Before he left the center for the day, Sam decided to look up Barclay's Bank where Maryanne worked. Bank hours on Friday were later than other days, and he wondered if she would be interested in having dinner with him. He called the bank and was put on hold until she was free to speak.

"Oh, hi Sam, how are you?" Maryanne sounded delighted that he had called. "What do you need? I only have a few minutes to talk."

"I was wondering if you'd like to get a drink or dinner after work. I could meet you at the bank." Sam was hesitant now, realizing how clumsy he sounded. She probably already had plans for the entire weekend. "I mean, if you're free."

"Well, I am free. I'm off around 6:30, but I really have to go now because we have several customers waiting." Maryanne rang off, leaving Sam to wonder if they had a date for dinner or not. He would just have to turn up at the bank at 6:30.

In the meantime, Sam had a couple of hours to spare. He decided to rush home to get a quick shower and feed Harry before he drove back into the city. Harry was delighted to get some attention, wagging his tail, and jumping up. He obviously needed a walk. Sam got the leash, and they took off around the corner to the dog park where Harry could run for a while. Sitting on a bench watching the dogs chase each other, Sam called his father.

Alan's phone went to voicemail, so Sam left a message. "Hey, Dad, it's me. I'm taking Harry to the park and then I'm going to be out for a while. Just thought you'd like to know. Hope your investigation is going okay. We can catch up over the weekend. Bye."

Walking Harry home, Sam considered again how he would quit using the Adderall. If he attended a local meeting, he knew he would find support networks and probably a sponsor. He wondered just how much Carla and his father suspected he had a problem.

At 6:30, Sam was sitting on a bench in the open courtyard when Maryanne walked out the bank door. He had flowers next to him and he was reading something on his phone. She walked carefully over and sat quietly beside him.

"Oh!" Sam was startled. "I didn't see you at the door. How was work?"

"Do you always sit on a bench with flowers on a Friday evening? Are you expecting anyone special?"

Sam was embarrassed. He picked up the flowers and gave them to her. "I thought you deserved these after all you've been through. Do you have time for dinner?"

Maryanne laughed and took the flowers. "Thank you. Yes, it would be great to have dinner. I was feeling a bit nervous about walking home anyway. I can't help thinking about the guy who died in the fire."

"Let's go find someplace and start with a glass of wine," Sam suggested as he held out his arm to her. "How about the Copley again? It's close to your studio and I can make sure you get home safe."

They found a quiet table in a little bistro at Copley Plaza. Sam wanted to learn more about Maryanne and keep the discussion away from the fire and Marko's death. He asked her about growing up on the West Coast and if it was true that everyone had a horse.

"Of course not! Why do people on the East Coast think we're all cowboys out west? And another thing, why do people ask me if I know someone who lives in Washington as if there are only a few of us living there? It's so frustrating! Some people even refer to me as 'the girl from Spokane' as if I'm the only one!"

They both laughed. Ordering a second glass of wine and crab cakes, the conversation became easier. Sam shared his years of study and travel which Maryanne envied. She told him that she wanted to see more of the East Coast before she returned home. Manhattan, Cape Cod, DC, and Maine were all the places she intended to visit. She had already experienced a glorious autumn while living in rural Massachusetts, and she looked forward to other wonderful adventures.

"What are your plans, Sam? Will you stay with your father for now? You asked me about renting a place on my street, but you need to know the rents are high. I was lucky to get my little studio."

Sam reluctantly admitted that living with his father was not ideal. "I'm used to a lot of independence and not having to keep a schedule. I guess that's going to change anyway now that I have a job."

"Is your father pretty set in his ways? I know both my father and mother would be horrible to live with. They had rules for us that I'm sure they just made up to keep us confused."

Sam reassured Maryanne that his father was easy going. "He's devoted to his work and keeps odd hours. I've been trying to make dinners, but I never know when he's going to walk through the door. Now I sound like I'm his wife!" Sam and Maryanne laughed at the thought.

Sam pulled out his phone and showed her a photo of Harry with a leash in his mouth. "At least I know Harry likes having me home."

They eventually noticed it was close to ten o'clock. Sam paid the bill and walked Maryanne home. On the way, she pointed out Tony's shop and told Sam how much she depended on this older man for news of the street. Not wanting to assume too much, Sam asked Maryanne what her plans were for the weekend. She gave him her phone number and said he could call. Once again, she was not committing to anything.

# SATURDAY, MAY 21<sup>ST</sup>

Enrique loved the weekends being at home with his family. His wife, Marie, never liked living in the city and so a couple years ago they bought a small two-story older home in Dorchester. They knew the school district had high standards which they preferred for their three girls who were now elementary age. Even though it took him hours sometimes to fight traffic home, Enrique enjoyed the feel of living in a neighborhood.

Marie understood when Enrique was called away for work, but this Saturday was the Block Watch BBQ and he had promised to be home. Rubbing at her temples, Marie questioned him, "Can't you at least get home for the potluck? We were counting on you to cook the meat."

Opening his mouth to respond, Enrique paused to collect his thoughts. He seldom worried Marie about the cases he was investigating, and now was no different. "I'll try to be back by five. I promise."

Marie looked sharply at him, "You know I hate that phrase. People promise things they know they cannot ever keep. Shows on TV are always saying they promise this or that and never... ever... do what they say!"

"Marie," Enrique slowly approached his wife with his arms out. She leaned into him and felt the comfort of his embrace. "You know I want to be with you and the girls. I have a few interviews to get through and then plan to meet Alan back at the office at one o'clock. When I'm done there, I'll drive back home."

Marie quickly kissed her husband, "Go now and get back here as soon as you can."

Enrique had contacted two of Marko's friends from the dinner parties he often hosted and was planning to meet them around ten. Teddy and Michael were both working at a restaurant near the market in the city. Finding an easy parking place on the street for once, Enrique walked the few blocks to the restaurant. He saw two guys sitting at a small table outside who looked up as Enrique approached.

"Teddy and Michael?" Enrique asked as he held out his hand. Both guys stood up as Enrique showed them his badge. Teddy was a light caramel colored Latino with thick black hair. He had fashionable black glasses and wore expensive shoes. Michael looked like a contradiction with his long blond ponytail and sneakers. Both were about the same height as Enrique.

"Thanks for meeting with me today. I wanted to ask you about Marko Miller. How long have you been friends with him?" Both guys looked at one another and questioned when they had met Marko. Enrique watched as they shrugged their shoulders in unison and tilted their heads. They agreed it was probably a year ago when Jerome introduced them.

"When was the last time you saw Marko?" Enrique continued his probing. Once again, the two friends checked with one another. Finally, Teddy said, "Marko came to the theater the night before he died. It was his big show and a huge success. We all planned to celebrate with him the following week." Teddy shook his head back and forth, "I just can't believe he's dead. This doesn't make any sense to me."

Enrique asked if they knew anything about Marko's personal life.

Teddy answered, "Everyone liked Marko. As far as I know he didn't go to a gym, but he liked to jog along the Charles a couple days a week. He was in great shape. And I don't think he belonged to any clubs because he was so busy with two or three jobs. What do you think, Michael?"

"I don't know of any clubs, or if he belonged to anything else. He didn't seem like a joiner to me. Did you ask Jerome? He was his best friend, you know. We all just tagged along for the parties and the decent conversation. Hey... maybe Marko took classes. He was always talking about traveling and making plans to visit some exotic jungles."

Teddy nodded, "That's right! When we got together to celebrate another one of his statues, he always had way too much information about the places they could be found and what they ate and how they survived. He had a real talent for making it interesting."

Enrique asked about a possible relationship Marko

might have had and both men said they didn't know. "It's funny, isn't it?" Michael thought, "We never knew if he was seeing anyone. When we brought it up, he'd just laugh and ignore us." Because he was a well-trained detective, Enrique had a habit of scanning the mannerisms of others and paying close attention to body language. At this point of the interview, he had no doubt that the two men were telling the truth. He thanked them for talking with him and, checking his watch, he was right on time to meet with Alan.

Working seven days a week during a murder investigation was nothing new to Alan. He insisted on following the details of the case as closely as possible, as if it were a novel he was devouring. Arriving at the office with strong black coffee and a low-calorie raisin roll, Alan collected the information about Marko's bank, savings and checking accounts, that the tech people had sent over. It looked like Marko had a healthy savings and his bills were up to date. His paychecks from the teen center and drag company were enough to keep him comfortable, but it looked like he made over twice as much designing gowns. Thinking about Alicia's employing Marko, Alan wondered if she only paid him in cash since he didn't see any deposits from her store.

Sipping his coffee, Alan began mentally running through everything known about Marko. He appeared on the outside to be an upright citizen who was doing more than enough to help friends and clients. But nobody seemed to know much more about him on a personal level. What could he have been doing on Saturday? Alan would wait and talk with Enrique at one o'clock as planned. In the meantime, he would look over the arson report that had finally been released.

When Enrique arrived, he was relieved to find Alan already at his desk. Maybe he would make the BBQ after all. "Hey, boss, how're you doing today?" Enrique smiled and nodded his head to Alan. "I just came from interviewing two of Marko's friends. Nice guys, but they don't know anything. Both Teddy and Michael were oblivious to Marko's personal life except for the parties they attended. Did you learn anything new?"

"Nope. All his bills are paid, and he had a comfortable savings account. I didn't even find a calendar, except for work, or any mention of activities that kept him busy. It looks like he read quite a bit about exotic animals and places to visit, but he didn't have plans to travel as far as I could see. It's very odd."

Enrique stood and walked over to the incident board. Usually, the facts, remarks, comments, and observations on the board pointed the way to a link. It was like the idea of seeing the wood instead of the trees. "Wait, we're assuming he was killed at the building, what if he was killed somewhere else and his body was just dumped there because they knew they were going to burn the place down? We don't have any forensic evidence that he was actually killed there."

But everything he saw on the board only pointed to Marko's two, or three, jobs, and all the people involved with his work. "Do you think he had some sort of secret life? Maybe he had a relationship with someone who was married or was keeping a low profile for some untoward reason." Enrique slumped back into the chair and sighed. "Where do we go from here?"

They seemed to be back to square one. Alan handed the arson report to Enrique and noted that it was clear someone had intended to do real damage. The fire inspector had agreed to meet with them to go over the report. They also needed the names of those who lived in the apartments and, maybe, who would get the most out of burning the place down. These might be separate cases. What if Marko had been dead when the place was set on fire?

Alan was meeting with the building owner early Monday morning. Hopefully, he would get the name of the manager for the building and a list of occupants. He also wanted to get the name of the exterminating company. In the meantime, he insisted that Enrique go home and enjoy his family.

Sidney had been up the night before thinking about his brother and wishing he had kept more in touch. Perhaps his regrets came from a long understanding about himself—that he shied away from intimate involvement or commitment. This had been true at work and certainly in his personal life. If he didn't get too close to people, he didn't have to worry about revealing his inner thoughts or feelings. Walking around his spacious townhouse, Sidney was overcome with a feeling of unease. Was he too old to change his ways now? This thought remained lodged at the back of his mind, causing him to be restless.

Picking up his iPad, he scrolled through his recent music playlists and then decided to listen to some oldies. Ray Charles was always one of his favorites, and when he saw the song "It was a very good year" with Willie Nelson, Sidney felt even more disheartened. He was that old man now. At 63, what did he have to say for himself? What had he accomplished? He realized how few friends he had. In fact, did he have a friend? All he did was work and come home. Even on the weekends he worked. He struggled to recall his last vacation. The only time, recently, was when he went away to a legal conference in Nassau. He enjoyed the sun and beach, but mostly concentrated on the work.

Sidney was beginning to recognize how much he missed companionship. He dated off and on over the years, but no relationship really took. He'd considered marrying one bright and beautiful law clerk, but she left him when he didn't show up for her family's reunion. Well, he knew that wasn't the only reason. He wasn't a great listener. If anything, he required that people get to the point of what they wanted so he could get back to work. What a fool he was.

His siblings had called several times over the week and offered to help Sidney clear out Marko's condo. They seemed especially impressed with the collection of statues and kitchen appliances that Marko had purchased over the years. Each one expressed the idea of having a statue to remember their brother by. Sidney liked that idea, but he was putting off visitors or a memorial until the police were finished with the investigation. Maybe today he should try to pack up the books and clothes from the condo.

Just as Sidney was walking out the door around three o'clock, his phone rang. It was Detective Sharp wondering if Sidney had time for coffee. This lightened Sidney's mood immensely, even considering that the detective would probably be asking more questions about Marko that he couldn't answer. Sidney stepped outside to a beautiful day. The air held his attention as he breathed in the scent of mowed lawn. Even the small patches of grass along the sidewalks had been freshly mowed. Sidney felt a surge of redemption. He hoped he could change his life and his attitude.

Saturdays in the city of Boston were crowded with tourists and Boston Red Sox fans. Fenway Park was one of the most popular attractions in the area, especially when there was a game. The Market was also busy, especially on weekends, and the thought of finding a decent place for coffee in the city was a joke. Sidney mentioned to Alan that he was on his way to Marko's condo and so they agreed to meet at a small coffee shop close to that address. It had outside seating and with a day like this day, it was preferred.

Alan had already selected a table when he saw Sidney approaching. Shaking hands, both men sat and commented on the weather. They were not good at small talk but were making the effort.

"Do you do any exercise Detective?" Sidney lowered his head and then smiled up at Alan.

"Well, let's see. Does walking my dog two blocks to the park each day count?" Alan smiled. "I wish I had more discipline. I used to jog if you can believe it. But that was years ago. Now I just watch my middle grow and avoid stairs." Alan sat back and felt a little embarrassed. Sidney looked in great shape. "How about you? What do you do to keep so trim?"

"It's all in the gene's, Detective. I wish I could tell you that I have a trainer and work out regularly. But truthfully, the only thing I've done different lately is walk a mile or two to work on beautiful days like this." Sidney lounged on his chair and found talking to Alan very comfortable.

"I guess I should walk more too," Alan observed. "And, by the way, please call me Alan. I'm sure that Marko would like us to be friends." Sidney nodded his head in agreement.

After ordering coffee and a sandwich, the two men began to piece together information about Marko that might make a difference to the investigation. Alan related his frustration about not knowing what Marko did in his free time. There was no record of activities or relationships. He had his friends, of course, but they didn't know about his life away from them either.

Sidney shook his head and then offered, "I'm going over to the condo after we finish here. Maybe I'll find some clue that we might have missed."

Alan appreciated the help and asked Sidney to keep in touch. They parted around 4:30 and Alan had to decide what he would do next.

Maybe he would see if Sam was home and wanted to do something. He noticed that Sam had arrived home late the night before and was still sleeping when he left for the office at eight. Alan needed to remember to ask him what he had been doing, but then scratched his head and realized he had no right to pry. Once again, he was bemused by the unspoken rules between them.

Sam had been surprised when he got up that morning to see his father had already gone. He was hoping to talk about the case some more so he would have a reason to call Maryanne. When Alan still hadn't returned at 1:00, Sam called her anyway to see if she would like to take a walk.

"I'm just going out," Maryanne laughed when she heard Sam's voice. "Saturdays are my catchup days when I have a chance to shop and do laundry. It's really boring, but if I get things done then I'm free all-day Sunday."

"How about tomorrow then? The weather looks great both days." Sam wondered if he sounded like a desperate guy, begging for attention. "If you're free, that is. I may have more information about the case by then." Now he felt stupid. "I mean, if you want to know more." At this point Sam felt like hanging up the phone and losing her number.

Maryanne continued to laugh. "Sam, you are so transparent. I'd love to go for a walk tomorrow. How about 11:00 and we can have lunch, too."

When Sam hung up, he slid down on to the floor with his hands holding his head. The last time he had a girlfriend was a year ago and he wasn't such an idiot. In fact, they got along so well people thought they were related. But they parted ways when the year was over, each accepting scholarships in different parts of the country. To calm his nerves, Sam decided to take Harry for a long walk.

Alan returned home to find Sam lounging on the sofa

in front of the television. "I missed you this morning! I decided to get some work done at the office. How are you doing?"

Sam turned down the sound on his show and smiled at his father. "Harry and I went for a long walk today. I think it did us both some good because we're exhausted." Alan looked at Harry who was sprawled out on the floor.

"He really needed that. I just don't give him enough attention these days. Speaking of attention, do you want to go to a movie or do anything else tonight? I'm taking time off from the case for at least 12 hours and trying to distract myself. We could have a bite to eat too." Alan eased into the overstuffed chair near the sofa. He really had the desire to sleep, but the look on Sam's face indicated that he liked the idea of going somewhere.

"A movie would be great. There's the old theater downtown that shows classics. Do you want to go there? I think the show this time is a western." Sam knew his father loved westerns. Alan agreed and they decided to leave in an hour.

Retreating to his room, Alan collapsed on the bed, not realizing how exhausted he was. As he closed his eyes, he tried to forget the details of his case, but Marko's face kept coming into his memory. Everybody liked him. Who would want to kill him? As he pondered these questions, he slowly fell asleep.

An hour and a half later, Sam knocked gently on his father's door. Jerking awake, Alan muttered, "Yes, what time is it?" He hadn't meant to fall asleep and was embarrassed that Sam had found him lying down. Sitting up and rubbing his face, Alan smiled sheepishly at his son, "I guess I was more tired than I thought."

"Do you still want to go to the movie? We don't have to, in fact, I'll go and get us a pizza and we can watch something on TV."

Appreciating the offer, Alan thought it was probably a good idea. His sleepless nights were obviously catching up with him and he didn't trust he would be able to stay awake in the theater. Giving Sam some cash, he suggested he also stop and get the new James Bond movie that was just out on DVD. They both loved the Bond characters and this one had great reviews.

While Sam was out, Alan washed his face in cold water and grabbed a beer. Having Sam around may turn out okay. What would he be doing on a Saturday night anyway? Working on a case? Reading reports? His life had certainly become mundane. Maybe he needed a hobby or could take a class like other seniors do. Where did all those seniors hang out? They probably all golfed. He needed a buddy. Where had all his friends gone? Sam returned as Alan's reverie stopped without giving him any answers.

The pepperoni pizza was amazingly greasy and delicious. It reminded Alan of his college days when pizza was gulped down with pitchers of beer. He looked at Sam and asked, "Do kids today spend hours eating pizzas and guzzling beers on weekends?"

"I suppose," Sam thought. "I never had enough time to spend in pizza parlors. If I wasn't doing homework, I was working at my job in the art room to keep my scholarship. The art department was so backed up with matting and hanging work that I was busy all of the time." Alan watched his son and wondered if he had been happy at school. The thought of drugs also crossed his mind.

"Was it too much? Working and schoolwork both taking up so much of your time. I thought you had a girlfriend, too."

Sam laughed for a minute. "I did. But we weren't as serious about a relationship as we were about getting through school. She's out in California now finishing her degree in communications. We'll probably see her one day as a field correspondent on some news show." Alan smiled at Sam. His son sounded content with how things worked out.

After enjoying the movie together, Sam and Alan stumbled to their rooms. James Bond had once again saved the world from another villain, and they would be able to sleep in peace tonight.

# SUNDAY, MAY 22<sup>ND</sup>

Alan was up early the next morning and feeling rested. He had already taken Harry for a walk and was having his second cup of coffee when Sam walked into the kitchen. He was dressed in his sweats and announced that he would begin jogging today. "If I'm going to be sitting at a desk all day, I better get some exercise. Do you want to go with me?" They both laughed.

Today Alan decided to return to St. Botolph Street to see if any of the owners of the neighboring buildings were around. He also wanted to speak with the patrol officers who knew this area to find out about the drug traffic. Calling ahead to the precinct nearby the street, he was put in touch with Officer Daly and Officer Parker. They would meet him around 11:00 at the damaged building.

Sam had made plans with Maryanne at exactly that same hour and was just rounding the corner to her building when he saw his father. Alan had parked his car and turned to look down the street from the corner of the block when he met Sam's eyes. Walking quickly to meet each other, Alan was the first to speak, "What are you doing here?"

"I have a date with Maryanne Collier, she lives here." Sam sheepishly said, his face instantly flushing. "I was going to tell you last night, but you were really tired, and so I decided to let it go."

"How do you know her?" Alan felt his curiosity awakened and his heart rate picking up. Letting out a deep breath, he stepped back and tried to appear unmoved.

Sam ran his fingers through his hair and apologized. "I'm sorry I didn't tell you before. I met Maryanne this week when I was waiting for you to have lunch. And then we had dinner on Friday after work. We kind of hit it off and so today we're going for a walk." Sam bit his lip. "Sorry, Dad."

Alan shrugged and patted Sam on the shoulder. "No, I'm the one to apologize. You have a personal life after all. Just be sure you don't get in the way of the case, okay? A lot of folks around here would like to know more about the investigation, but we're keeping a low profile for now."

Sam agreed and looked at his watch. He was already late, and when he saw his father look at the time also, he realized they would have to continue this conversation another time. They both walked quickly to their destinations.

Maryanne was waiting at the door and had seen the two men talking. As she let Sam into her studio she chided, "What's up? It looked like you and your father were in quite a serious discussion. Does he not approve of his son meeting with someone on this street?"

"No, he's okay." Sam was staring at Maryanne's tiny space. It was only one room with a small kitchenette not even big enough for a table and chair. The bathroom door was slightly open, and it looked as though you could barely stand up in the room. "Where's all your stuff? I mean, this is so small." Sam realized, once again, he was making assumptions and quickly tried to recover. "You must be a minimalist. I have more junk in my closet than you do here." By the look on Maryanne's face, his heartbeat began to race, and he felt his face turning warm. "Oh man, I'm really not saying this right. I'm sorry to be so rude."

Maryanne sat down on her sofa, which was also her fold out bed, and stared up at Sam. "I left my ex with only my clothes and essentials. I don't want to accumulate much of anything when I know I'll be moving again. Remember? I'm returning to the West Coast in a year."

Sam sat down next to her and took her hand. "I'm sorry for how that sounded. I understand your situation. I guess I just didn't really think about what it means to have to leave everything behind and start over." Looking carefully for Maryanne's reaction, Sam saw tears in her eyes. He reached over and put his arm around her, surprised by her sudden emotion.

"I'm just getting by Sam. My divorce isn't even final yet and I've asked for nothing from my ex. I just want out. He's a vindictive person and will take me to court if I don't just walk away. If I had known he had that side to his personality, I never would have married him." Flustered now by saying too much, Maryanne quickly stood up and put on her sweater.

"Let's go for our walk."

Sam jumped up and held out his hand. "Good idea. I thought we might have lunch along the Charles after our walk. I heard there was a great Pho place." Sam hoped his decision not to press Maryanne for details about her former life was a good idea. It didn't appear that she wanted to talk about it, anyway.

Alan was confused. Of all the people Sam could have met in such a short time, why did it have to be this girl? He could brush this off as fate or a coincidence, but he wanted to be reassured this new information wouldn't impact his case. Maybe his mind was going to the worse-case scenario. He would talk with Sam later and set out some boundaries. But for the time being, he had more immediate concerns.

The two police officers were waiting to meet him at the building site. One officer looked like he just graduated from High School and the other was approaching middle age. It was typical of the precinct to pair officers with experience and trainees together. Usually, the rookie had a better grip on the rapidly changing technology that was fast overtaking the department, while the veteran had the street smarts that came from years on the force. Alan shook hands with both men. "I need some information about the drug activity around here. I understand this specific address has a rep for drug deals. What can you tell me?"

Officer Parker spoke first, "We generally see a lot of teens and early twenties hanging around here. The drugs of choice are usually street stuff like weed, pills, and heroin." The younger officer broke in, "There's also oxy and even Adderall for sale sometimes. Stuff you usually find in the schools, but we've noticed it's working its way onto the streets on a larger scale than before. We've busted a few users, but they're afraid to I.D. the dealers. I've seen kids as young as twelve out here who I've suspected of dealing." He shook his head and pursed his lips.

Once again Officer Parker spoke, "We're starting to see a pattern. The dealers are getting more sophisticated. The bad guys are using young kids as mules to deliver the goods to the buyers or selling out of small businesses where lots of traffic isn't so noticeable. We suspect someone who lives in this building is dealing, but we're not sure who it is. We're trying to keep tabs on who's coming and going, but we haven't been able to spot anyone yet. One thing for sure, they're not doing sidewalk sales. Whoever it is, is pretty savvy, and knows to stay out of sight. We don't see the open activity you see in some other areas. That would be spotted here in a heartbeat. But something's going on for sure."

"Can you give me the names of the dealers?" Alan took his note pad out to write down any information they might have.

"We're investigating a few people in the area. One has ties to this building, and another keeps such a low profile that we don't have a name or address." They gave Alan the name Henry Olson, a suspected dealer working for the Boston Utilities Company. Alan thanked them and gave them his card. His mind was skipping ahead to possible new insights on how and where drug dealers lived and worked. He decided to return to the precinct and do some research.

Just as Alan was entering the office, his phone rang. Surprised by the call on a Sunday, Alan answered casually. "Sharp here."

"Detective, this is Alicia Grant. I guess I'm surprised you answered your phone."

Alan held his breath for a minute, not knowing how to respond, then said, "What can I do for you Ms. Grant?"

"Please call me Alicia to start with. I just need to know if you have made any progress on the case. I have spoken to several of my clients, and they didn't have a clue how to help. It's so typical of the elite, not wanting to get involved."

"Thank you for your help, Alicia, but I'm not at liberty to discuss an ongoing case with you."

"I understand, Detective. Can I give you the name of the last customer Marko was working with? Maybe she heard something from Marko that will mean something to you."

"Yes, please do." Alan was pleased to have a new person who might know more about Marko.

"Her name is Nancy Quinn. Do you want her number?"

Alan wrote the phone number down, thanked Alicia and hung up. It looked like she was not going to give up following this investigation. He didn't know if he was annoyed or pleased when his phone rang again.

"Alan, this is Sidney Miller. I'm over at Marko's condo today and I think I know what he was doing on weekends and probably some evenings. If you would like, I can come to the precinct and bring what I've found." Sidney's willingness to help take on the responsibility of assisting with the investigation pleased Alan. He said he would be waiting for him.

While waiting, Alan went to his computer and pulled up the incident-location files of police callouts for the block of St Botolph St. covering the past year. He wasn't surprised to see there were several incidents logged at the address. Quite a few noise complaints, a couple of simple assaults and several "drug possession/sales". In addition, there was one "threat to do bodily harm", "a sick assist—drug related", as well as a mix of "verbal disputes", "vandalism" and calls to "investigate a person." All of this fit with what his witnesses had told him about the building.

When Sidney arrived, Alan was just completing a call from Carla. She wanted an update on Marko's investigation and was frustrated that she couldn't help more. Alan heard the sadness in her voice and promised to call her when he had more information.

"Sidney, tell me what you know." Alan rose slightly from his chair and offered a folding chair next to his desk. Sidney sat quickly and produced a packet of mail from the bag he was carrying. "I found a key for a mailbox that obviously belonged to Marko. The nearest post office was only a couple of blocks away and when I tried the number on the key it opened the box and mail fell out. At first, I thought it was only junk mail, but when I sorted through, I found this letter. I almost tossed it, but it appeared to be personal." He handed the letter to Alan.

It was from a local gym that ran programs for kids who needed a place to go. It looked like Marko was forming a basketball team for teens and the letter informed him that thirty kids had signed up.

Almost rendered speechless, both men stared at one another. "What does this mean?" Sidney spoke in a whisper. "I am awe struck. I'm finding out more about my brother than I have ever known before and feel ashamed. He is…was… remarkable." Sidney rubbed the back of his neck and shook his head.

Alan nodded, "Well, I can tell you this, it does match up with the Marko I knew. He always wanted to do more for people, always put them first. I'm glad you brought this to my attention. I'll go to this gym tomorrow and see if they can give me any information about Marko's connections there."

"What now, Alan?" Sidney sat back and let his shoulders drop. "Wait until I tell my family about Marko. They will want to canonize him. I just wish I had stopped being my arrogant and superior self and took the time to get to know him better. He was talented, compassionate, fun-loving, and worked with teens with addictions. Who does this? And who in their right mind would want to kill him?"

Alan thought out loud, "People like Marko make me feel good about being human, about being alive at a time when someone like him is around." Both men agreed. Alan continued, "Where do we go from here? I need to go back to the files. Perhaps I dismissed something as unimportant and will find that it's a tiny but crucial part of the case. Somewhere in all the documents and interviews there might be a remark or an innuendo or something I wondered about that will point me in the right direction."

Sidney shook his head slightly, "Please let me know

what you find. Anything you can tell me about my brother I appreciate." Alan smiled in agreement. He liked Sidney and hoped they might continue a friendship.

# MONDAY, MAY 23<sup>RD</sup>

Sam woke early to take a run before work. His mind was drifting to Maryanne and how much he liked being with her. Yesterday they had walked miles along the Charles River and watched the singing oarsmen from the Harvard Rowing Crew sculling down the river. Their conversation had finally taken a lighter note and they laughed about movies and friends and families. He was in awe of her large family, and she sometimes wished she could have been an only child. Both were avid readers and shared book titles and authors. Maryanne preferred historical novels and Sam devoured mysteries. By the time they returned to St Botolph Street they agreed to meet up during the week for pizza. Sam was looking forward to it.

Walking through the door from his run, Sam met his father in the kitchen. Settling into his first cup of coffee, Alan motioned for Sam to have a seat. "We need to establish some rules," he began. "I need to know that our paths don't cross when I am in the middle of an investigation." Alan paused for a moment and narrowed his eyes as if intense concentration would give him a glimpse of where he would take this conversation without sounding overbearing. "You knew the building that burned was on the street where Maryanne lives, and so it would have been wise to let me know you had met her. I realize what a coincidence this could have been, but anything that touches this case will be scrutinized—and the police don't believe in coincidences. Can you understand this?"

Sam stared at his father. "If I thought she was part of the investigation, I would have said something earlier. But, Dad, you haven't exactly been home. And when you are home, you're so exhausted. Now since I have a job with Carla, what if something comes up? Should I tell you about it? Or maybe not tell you because it's confidential information. What do you want me to do?"

Alan turned his head to one side and thought for a moment. Sam was right. He would have to think about all of this. "I see what you mean, Sam. Sorry if you think I doubt you, or maybe I just doubt myself. If our paths do intersect, I guess we'll have to expect it. Let's keep our minds open to the fact that this might happen." Turning to rinse his coffee mug in the sink, Alan wondered if he had said the right thing. He didn't want to lose Sam's trust now.

"Good luck at work today," Alan yelled as Sam ran up the stairs to get a shower.

The name of the gym found on the letter to Marko was Anderson Fitness Center. It was an old establishment in the heart of Roxbury run by a former NBA basketball player who played pro in the eighties. He had opened the gym to encourage teens to work out their anger, or channel their energy, onto the basketball court. Over the years he had helped develop intermural teams noted for their skills and their abilities to work together. The trophies in the display case were testaments to hard work.

Cal Anderson met Alan with a smile. He was 6'4" and still had the build of a pro-player. He walked with a slight limp due to crushing his ankle two times on court. Although it ended his basketball career, it didn't seem to stop his energy for sports. He led Alan into his very small office and pushed papers off a foldup chair and asked him to sit. Cal sat beside his small desk.

"I am absolutely stricken to hear about Marko's death. What can I do to help you, Detective?"

"We found a letter from you about a basketball team Marko was apparently starting or sponsoring. Can you tell me about that?"

"Marko and I had discussed forming a team with the kids he worked with at the center. It would be co-ed which was a great idea when you think about it. He wanted to encourage girls to compete and have a sense of their own abilities and talents. When we put the idea out there, a number of teens signed up."

"When was the last time you spoke with Marko?"

"The weekend before he died, I guess. We went to lunch and then hung fliers around for interested teens. That was why I sent him the letter, to officially let him know we were successful. Hey, did you find his wallet? He left it at the gym and when I couldn't get a hold of him, I just mailed it."

"Yes, we did get the wallet. Thanks. When you spoke to him, did he express any concerns or problems he was having with anything or anyone?"

Cal sat and thought for a minute. He stood up and went to a file cabinet next to the door. "I have the list of teens who signed up if this helps. But Marko didn't say if he was worried about any of them. At least, not to me." Handing over the list, Alan noticed that Eddie Pearson's name was on it.

"Do you know Eddie Pearson?"

"He's been in here a couple of times. Each time he gets out of rehab his father always gives him a couple months at the gym to work on his issues. He starts a session and then he gives up. I was surprised to see his name of this list."

Alan noticed the time on the wall clock and realized he had to leave for his next appointment. Thanking Cal, he handed him his card and asked him to call if he thought of anything else. Cal smiled, "Just like in the movies, right?"

Reagan Realty was located near Cambridge in an old three-story Victorian building. Constructed of rusticated stone with rough surfaces, Alan thought it resembled the Trinity Church in Boston. His father would probably know all about the architecture and who influenced this style. Alan appreciated how so many old buildings had survived the growth of the city and continued to remind people of the grandness of earlier centuries.

His meeting with David Reagan was scheduled for ten o'clock and he was on time. A young woman, sitting at a reception desk and smartly dressed in a navy ensemble, greeted Alan as he walked through the ornate door. After checking her appointments diary, she immediately escorted him into Reagan's office. High ceilings and light grey walls gave a spacious feel to the office which was grounded by dark hardwood floors. Two antique bookcases dominated one wall and ornately framed paintings of seascapes hung over the elegant desk centered on an adjacent wall. Alan was impressed, but not overwhelmed because he could only imagine how much they paid in rent.

David Reagan, who appeared to be in his early seventies, pushed his bulky weight up from his ample desk chair and offered his hand to Alan. Reagan was prosperously heavy, with a round face, longish white hair, white eyebrows, and wearing a custom-made black pin-striped tailored suit. His shirt was stark white and stretched across his successful middle. He looked to Alan like a heart attack waiting to happen.

Alan got right to the point, as usual. "Your building on St. Botolph Street is the subject of an arson investigation, as you probably know. We're investigating a body, found inside the building after the fire, as a probable homicide. I would like the names of the tenants in the building. Also, we're curious why all the tenants were gone from their homes on this particular weekend." Stopping at this point to give time for a response, Alan sat back and retrieved his notebook and pen from his coat pocket.

"I was distressed to hear about the fire and even more upset when I heard someone had died there." Reagan sat heavily down on his chair. "I do have an explanation about the tenants, Detective. There have been problems with rats and bugs infiltrating the apartments and I wanted to do something about it. I asked all the tenants to leave for the weekend so I could get an exterminator in to take care of the problem. Thank God they were all out of the building! I will give you the names of the tenants and I certainly hope one of them was not the person who died." Reagan shuffled through files on his desk and finally came to the one he wanted. Handing it to Alan, he stood up to indicate the meeting was now over.

"I have a few more questions, Mr. Reagan." Alan looked seriously at the older man. "I heard from Mr. Quinn that this building was insured for well over the appreciated value. What was your reasoning for this?"

Reagan put his hands in his pockets and looked down at Alan, "Now, Detective, you know yourself that prices are rising all over the city. It was foresight on my part to buy more insurance than necessary on that building. Once I have the money from the insurance, I'll need most of it to rebuild. And with the costs of permits, contractors and building supplies these days, I'd be lucky to break even." Reagan again attempted to end the conversation. "Please let me know how the investigation is proceeding. I would like to get started on rebuilding soon." Once again, he offered his hand.

Alan took his time putting his note pad away. He looked around at the high-priced office and slowly stood up. "I also need you to provide information about who manages the building and anyone else who services it. Can you think of who would want to set it on fire? Because, Mr. Reagan, this was definitely arson."

Reagan shuffled through more files on his desk and finally handed one to Alan. "I don't have a clue who would set it on fire. That's your job anyway and I would appreciate it if you spoke directly to the manager of the building, his information is in the file I just gave you. Thank you for coming in today, I have a client waiting." Reagan, beathing rapidly, sat and picked up his phone, dismissing Alan.

"One more question," Alan stared at Reagan, "who did you hire for the extermination?"

Reagan lowered his phone and let out a deep breath, "I'll have to get back to you on that. It's some private company outside the city I think." He stared at Alan to indicate the conversation was over.

As Alan walked back to his car, he wondered if he had missed something in the interview with Reagan. He knew it was easy to dismiss something as unimportant only to find out later it was an important piece of the puzzle. Why didn't he know the name of the exterminators?

Enrique was busy on his computer when Alan returned to the office. He was attempting to finish the reports from his interviews the previous day, before he had to hit the streets again. Alan greeted him with lowered brows and thoughts racing, trying to make sense out of all the information he had collected over the weekend. They both adjourned into Alan's office.

"Enrique, we're going to have to be careful to keep each other totally informed on this case. I'm beginning to get the feeling that our cross-checking is going to be very important. Let's re-read all the reports, check and re-check, crosscheck and discuss exhaustively everything we have so far to see what's missing." Frustration was showing as Alan paced the floor with his arms held tightly around his chest. Enrique listened attentively as Alan related his conversations with David Reagan and the two patrol officers. He also told him about meeting Cal Anderson at the gym that morning.

Enrique took in the information with a sigh. "I didn't really know Marko, but now I wish I did. Everyone liked him and no one knows who would want him dead. Everyone seems taken by surprise."

Alan decided to diagram the info they had collected and include all the witnesses and possible suspects. Using the incident board, he began to list the people he and Enrique had interviewed. He started with the interviews... Sidney, of course was not a suspect. And, for practical purposes, Jerome was also not suspected of being involved.

"I haven't had a chance to meet with Alicia Grant yet," Enrique reported.

"Okay, we don't really have any reason to suspect Alicia or Carla either. Let's look at the others."

Trudy was an unknown but suspicious. Both Alan and Jerome disliked Trudy. They knew she was lying about something and wondered about her finances. Since she was divorced and didn't have custody of her child, they doubted she had income from her ex. Her job at the department store was an unlikely source of much income, so how could she afford to live at and maintain her building? They heard that her renters had already moved after the fire because of the smoke damage. She should be desperate to sell, and she appeared to be hiding something.

She said she knew Marko and had called him several times. But it didn't appear she had a motive to want him dead. Was she lying?

*Eddie.* Although Eddie had a lot of bravado that was annoying, he seemed upset Marko was dead. According to Carla, Marko was making progress with Eddie and had contacted a rehab for him. Eddie might know who was with Marko that night, especially if it was a drug dealer he used. They need to question him again.

*Les Quinn.* Again, no motive for him to be involved, as far as they knew insurance was his only business and the building was a loss for his company. He said he didn't even know Marko. Had never met him. But his wife, Nancy, knew Marko because he helped design some clothes for her at Alicia's store. It was a long shot, but maybe they needed to interview her.

*David Reagan.* He knew something about the building that he wasn't admitting. The whole idea about fumigating the place and having all the tenants leave for the weekend was too convenient. Maybe he was planning to burn the place down so he could finally get the cash he needed to turn it into someplace more profitable. Who were the people who worked for him? Alan had been given the name Henry Olson, an employee at the Boston Utility Company. Police said he hung around the building often and when they asked him why, he said he worked part time for the owner. Did he know Marko?

*Lily* was not a suspect—no apparent motive. Both men agreed on this. She seemed genuinely distressed to know Marko was dead.

*Tony* might know something more than he told them. Hopefully, he wasn't trying to solve this case on his own. He kept an eye out for drug dealers, and if they knew he was watching them, he might be in danger. He genuinely liked Marko and cared about finding who killed him.

Alan felt there was something lodged at the back of his mind that he couldn't put his finger on. Talking the case over with Enrique now helped him to clarify some thoughts. "Let's begin with the arson. It's one of the easiest crimes to get away with. We don't know who set the fire or why Marko was there. The fire department already looked for clues of arson, but they might have overlooked any personal items that the perpetrator may have left behind. Enrique, check with the forensic team and see what they turned up when they processed the scene."

Alan looked at his watch. "Let's go see the fire chief after we have lunch. I think going in person will get better results."

Trudy was furious! A whole week had gone by, and nobody could tell her about the investigation. When she spoke with her insurance agent about getting started on her remodel, he pressured her to calm down and wait for the appropriate paperwork to come through. Even though she had stashed away plenty of money from her drug sales, she was aware how suspicious it might look if she used it now for repairs on her building. Trudy had taken the week off from work to begin clearing out her clothes and anything of value, but the adjuster had even cautioned her against this. They needed to see all the damage before they could process the settlement.

Trudy thought about her years of practice deceiving people. The secrets and lies she guarded were so ingrained in her mind that she struggled to remember the truth sometimes. She was tired and stressed from her dealings with her suppliers, who seemed more threatening on each contact. She had to remain cautious and inform her contacts that any involvement with drugs now ran the risk of being uncovered by this ongoing investigation. It was time to lie low. Her primary dealer had not called her back. Where was he?

Standing now at the entrance of her building, she saw the two local officers who usually patrolled the neighborhood. She waved them down to continue her search for answers. "Officers, I'm very concerned about what's been happening to this neighborhood? I call you all the time about the noise and the drugs, but I never get a response. And now that building has burned down! What if my building was next? Or this whole block? We need answers!" Trudy was shaking and glaring at the men.

Officer Parker got out of the patrol car and leaned against the door. "Madam, we're in the process of investigating the fire. As far as we know, there's no threat to the neighborhood, but we've upped our patrols by several times each day. If you have any information, or receive any threats please call the precinct." Everybody at the station knew who this lady was and tried to avoid her calls. At first, they had followed up on her leads, but didn't find anything but some teens loitering. After a while, she was just annoying.

The two detectives were having burgers and cokes before meeting with the fire investigator who was handling the crime. "Do you know anything about how they evaluate the scene?" Enrique asked Alan.

"Well, the first thing they do is look for victims and remove anyone caught in the fire. That, of course, is a given. Then they try and determine the exact location where the fire started and what caused it. They also look for inflammable material and any ignition devices and ensure the building is safe." Alan thought for a moment, "I know they often try to interview any witnesses and bystanders who may have seen it begin. I don't know what happens next. We need to ask." Finishing his lunch, Alan glanced over to Enrique. "Ready?"

Fire Chief Joe Nolte was waiting at his desk when he saw the two detectives walk in. He was a seasoned fire investigator around sixty who had a lean build and curly gray hair. His smile was wide, and Alan noted how white his teeth were. After introductions, Alan got right to the point. "We'd like to know what you've concluded from your investigation of the Botolph Street fire, and we need to see what your team has discovered."

"Of course, Detective," Nolte agreed and took on an authoritative tone. "You know by now that we concluded the fire was arson. It started in the front hallway next to the body, although we found traces of the accelerant used, which was regular gasoline by-the-way, in two other places on the first floor of the building. We have pictures and videos you can look through for clues or evidence along with a written narrative, observations, and descriptions, as well as our detailed conclusions. This offers an unbiased roadmap for us and helps to refresh our minds."

"What about physical evidence? What do you do with that?"

"Before we can release the scene, we ensure that we have collected all possible evidence and documented it accurately. We identify, collect, and preserve any evidence to prevent contamination. Then we package, tag it and transport it to storage. This means we physically sift through the scene and collect any materials we deem relevant to the investigation. We're looking for anything that might be related to the fire. Since it was clear, early on, that the cause of this fire was suspicious, we suspected the death of the victim might also be, so we made sure your forensic team had access just as soon as we determined the building was safe to enter."

Nolte referred to a report he was holding, "In this

199

instance your homicide forensic team came in to process the body and do a thorough forensic search of the site before we removed the remains. So, there were two teams examining the location, although with slightly different focuses. As you know, fighting the fire was our priority, and high-pressure hoses can do a lot of damage to evidence, unfortunately."

Alan nodded in agreement. "We appreciate how thorough you are. Right now, we're focusing on the victim found at the scene. We'd like to see all the physical evidence you found on the first floor, and get copies of the photos, videos, and written reports." Nolte nodded and made a phone call. When he rang off, he told them it would take about an hour to gather the material they needed. Alan and Enrique retreated to chairs set up against the wall to wait.

When the detectives returned to the office later, they decided to divide up the work. Enrique offered to read through the fire investigators' reports and look through the evidence, while Alan reviewed the lists he received from Reagan. An hour later they both decided to take a break.

Alan poured himself a cup of stale coffee and put his feet up on his desk. "This is not looking very helpful," he said, pointing to the list of people. "Most of the tenants of that building were short term, some for as little as a month. You would think it was some sort of transitional housing, but I know Reagan wouldn't have gone along with any city programs like that. I called a few of these numbers but they were disconnected. So, the question is once again, what was Marko doing there? And did it have to do with drugs and dealing? Who, or what, was he looking for?"

"Going over the fire reports, it sure looks like arson," Enrique shook his head, letting go of any doubt he might have had. "I looked at the evidence they pulled from the first floor and besides coins and nails, the only items of interest were an earring, some sort of badge holder, part of a flashlight and some charred paperclips."

"Let me see the badge holder," Alan reached across his desk for the plastic bag. The holder was a bent metal frame with a pin attached. It could be anybody's, but there was something about the design that held his interest. "This is from an old I.D. I think. I remember when our mailman used to wear his personal nametag with a frame like this. You're so young, you would never recognize it." Alan winked at his young friend. "That's why you keep us old guys around, so we can recognize artifacts."

Enrique laughed, "Then why would it be in this building? If it's so old, why would someone use it now?"

"It could be for several reasons. It's an old building and it may have been left there for years. Or let's say someone found it and tried to pose as a delivery person, even a mailman. It might look professional, even though it's old school. Maybe it's a keepsake. You wouldn't believe some of the things I've held onto over the years. I still have my original social security card that came with a folder. I remember the first time HR saw it—they asked if they could take a picture of it!" Alan raised his eyebrows remembering how embarrassed he felt at the time.

"Do we have the evidence from forensics yet?"

Enrique spun in his chair and pulled over a storage box

that was sitting on the floor close to the door and removed the lid. Taking out the plastic bags which identified each item, they carefully compared them to the inventory list also inside the box. Most of the items were listed as found throughout the building. There was a hoop earring, a key, and a nail file. The fire department had listed the metal badge, a money holder, three penny's and two dimes, an AA coin, a St. Christopher medal, and nails that were probably from the walls. Nothing identified as the murder weapon.

"Was there anything else in the reports that looked suspicious?"

Enrique handed Alan the written forensic report of the site where the body was found. It was a multi-page report and contained several results from lab tests forensics had run on the various materials collected from the site, as well as specified parts of the building. They'd have to have a chat with forensics to clearly understand any implications of the test results.

In the report it appeared that Marko had been in front of an apartment door. Speculation might be that he knew who lived there and might not have been aware the building was empty. If everyone was gone, how did he get into building? Someone had to let him in unless he had a key. They looked through the list of tenants to find out whose apartment Marko was found in front of and if that person knew Marko. The name listed was P. Briggs. There was no phone number.

Alan frowned and narrowed his eyes as if intense concentration would reward him a glimpse of what had happened. So far not a scrap of evidence seemed directly connected to the murder. "Enrique, remember what I always say? No two individuals are alike. When two different people interview the same person, you can get two different results. I want you to set up an interview with David Reagan and find out what you can. I have a list of his service personnel and I need to know who works directly with him." Alan shifted in his seat and continued, "And I'm going to talk with Jerome and see if I can get more information about Marko."

Enrique reminded Alan that every Monday night was a big drag show and Jerome probably had a performance. He lived with his grandmother near the theater, so maybe Alan would have luck catching him at home. Alan reached for his phone and called Jerome.

Trudy was not satisfied with the policemen's casual response to her questions. She needed to speak with someone who had authority to make things happen, and that could only be the owner of the destroyed building. Riffling through papers in her desk, she finally came across the escrow papers for her building and found David Reagan's name. He had helped Trudy and her husband buy their building years ago. If she remembered correctly, he had interest in the building next to hers. Looking up the location for Reagan's company, she decided to visit him rather than phone. Even if he wasn't available, she would make it known that she wanted answers.

Thirty minutes later, Trudy was sitting in the office of the Reagan Realty Company. She wasn't intimidated by the young attractive receptionist who was busily typing on her laptop. Trudy did note that the grandness of the reception area was blurred by the few paintings on the wall showing scenes of battles that depicted soldiers falling to their knees. They didn't seem inviting to the public, and Trudy wondered who Reagan's clients might be.

David Reagan knew who Trudy was by reputation and decided to have her wait until he reviewed the sale of her building. It had been years ago, and he knew everything had been in order, but now he wanted to make sure. Her demands had been heard several times and with the arson attempt he wanted to be prepared for her confrontation. When he opened the door to invite her in, he could tell she was upset.

"How can I help you?" Reagan began, "I'm told you're concerned by the management of the insurance process. It's on my mind, too."

With mounting frustration, Trudy began to adjust her clothing and looked for a chair. Finding one by the door, she pulled it over to the massive desk and sat. She was not going to be put off by Reagan's superior manner. "I would like answers. When will the insurance money come through? Why is it taking so long?"

"I have no idea about your building, but my experience with insurance claims is that they take time."

Reagan calmly sat down across from her. "It's only been a week, my dear. Considering it's also a murder investigation, it will take even longer, I imagine. What can I do to help you?"

"I need the insurance money to fix up my building. My

three tenants have moved out because of the smoke and so my income from their rent will be gone. I was planning on selling in September, and now I don't have the money to begin remodeling." Trudy wrung her hands and tried to look helpless, hoping Reagan would understand how desperate she felt.

"Selling? Do you want me to make some calls for you and see if I can find a buyer? Sometimes we can sell 'as is' and get a very good price, especially on that street." Reagan was now eager to make a deal with Trudy. This was turning out in his favor after all. He asked Trudy if she would like some coffee or a soda.

Trudy smiled. This was more than what she had hoped for. Maybe she didn't have to deal with contractors and service people at all. She declined the coffee and sat to wait and hear what Reagan could offer her in the way of a sale. The faster she could put it on the market, the quicker she would be out of the city.

After reviewing the original sale of her building, Reagan said he would quietly ask around for interested buyers. He had a few acquaintances in mind, who might like to make an investment such as this. "The St. Botolph Street area has a reputation of growing appraisals, and the historic element alone makes it desirable. I'm certain I could get a very good price, especially if we move quickly." Reagan was pleased with this new project and hoped to make it worth his while.

With a fixed look of concentration, Trudy adjusted her thinking. "I have to contact my ex about selling before we move forward. I'll get back to you as soon as I do." Standing up and shaking hands with this pompous old man, she smiled devilishly. Trudy was delighted. If she could sell her building quickly, she could get out of the city and maybe even out of the country sooner than anticipated, and the safer she would feel. But first she had to talk it over with her ex and get him to sign papers. He was going to get Clara after all, so maybe he would be agreeable to selling the building now.

As soon as Trudy left the office, Reagan poured himself a drink and began to contemplate this new development. Maybe he could sell both buildings at the same time. The one that was destroyed could be billed as a potential add-on and become a sensational venture for one of his wealthy clients. He would have to investigate the historical mandates on permits for this area, but he knew housing and retail were the leading markets. Reagan decided to keep this all to himself while he made a study of possibilities. Hopefully, this lady would calm down and be patient.

Jerome agreed to meet with Alan around 5:30. This gave Alan enough time to rush home and check in with Sam and Harry. He was surprised to find Sam still not home and Harry rushing out the door once he opened it. "Well, I guess you need a walk." Alan looked in the usual place he kept the leash, and it wasn't there. Maybe it was in Sam's room.

Hating to intrude on his son's private space, Alan had no choice if he was going to have time for a walk. Sam's clothes were neatly folded on the dresser, quite a change from when he was a teenager. Alan smiled and looked for the leash. He found it next to the bed and noticed a bottle of pills on the nightstand. The prescription label was peeled off, but the bottle was almost full. Curious, Alan opened the cap to see what his son was taking. His knowledge of drugs made it clear that Sam had a bottle of Adderall. Alan's heart sank. No wonder he had noticed how thin Sam was and how much sleep he needed. These were both signs of drug use and it appeared Sam might be hiding an addiction.

Alan grabbed Harry's leash and closed the door to Sam's room. He wished he had a person to call and talk this over with. Carla would understand, but she was also Sam's boss now. Alan was going to have to deal with this on his own. He and Harry took off for the park and an hour later, Alan was back in his car and on the way to see Jerome.

The narrow house Alan parked in front of was built between two classic brownstones. It must have been a service entry or storage house before being rebuilt into the two-story cottage. Charming as it appeared, the lady who answered the door was even more gracious and, thought Alan, adorable. Her gray hair was wrapped in a colorful scarf with curls falling around her face. Bright eyes were dancing behind her red framed glasses and the warmth of her voice was endearing. Holding on to her sturdy walker, she invited Alan in. "We were expecting you, Detective. I'm Grandma Mae, please call me that. I don't think I've met a detective before and I'm 83!"

Alan walked slowly behind Grandma Mae who was dressed in a silk caftan painted with songbirds. The warm inviting sitting room was tastefully decorated. Although the furniture was old, it maintained an elegance of years gone by. The chintz sofa and matching chairs were centered around an antique looking table that held a steaming teapot and cups and saucers.

As Grandma sat in one of the chairs, her eyes searched the room for a minute, perhaps trying to remember something. She then laughed at herself, "It's so fun getting old. Every time I leave a room it takes me a while to recall what I wanted to do. Oh yes, now I know, Jerome is getting ready for his show tonight. He said he will hurry. Would you like some tea?"

Alan loved senior citizens like Mae. He hoped he would be just as lovable when he became forgetful and still enjoy some pleasures such as company and tea. "How long have you been here? Your home seems to be a kind of landmark, settled in between the two larger buildings."

"Well, let me remember the dates. My parents were the first owners of this house in the late 1800's. It wasn't much of a house then, just a one story shed-like structure. But my father was a wonderful carpenter and slowly, over the years, he built this house. My husband was pretty good with his hands, and he spent a lot of hours working on this place, too. Everything was updated again in the 50's." Mae stopped to take a sip of tea and seemed to be enjoying the memories. "Jerome, however, can't hammer a nail!"

"I can't do what?" Jerome entered the room with a flourish. He was so used to being onstage, that every movement seemed choreographed. He held out his hand whimsically for Alan and then sat down on the sofa beside him. "I hope that my grandmother has not been telling tales. She's been known to stretch the stories out and glamourize them." Jerome sent a kiss in the air across to Mae. "What can I help you with today, Detective?"

"I need to talk more about Marko. We've been looking for a reason why anyone would want to harm him. Did you know he was starting up a youth basketball team?" Both Mae and Jerome raised their eyebrows in unison.

"No!" Jerome was first to speak. "He never said a thing to me. Did you know this, Grandma?"

Mae shook her head, still in awe about what Alan said. "I knew he was busy most weekends, but I never thought it would be something like that."

Jerome reached inside a hidden pocket buried in the caftan and pulled out a key. "I found this in one of Marko's drawers at the studio. Maybe this is a key to the gym." He handed Alan what looked like a locker key.

Alan thanked Jerome and continued, "I want you to think again about anything Marko may have said or done that worried you. You and he were celebrating the Friday night before he died. Did he seem distracted?"

"I have thought about that night so many times." Jerome dabbed his eyes, not caring if his eye liner was ruined. "He always seemed worried about the teens he worked with. Our conversation that night was about the show at the club. But I remember he thought he saw someone he knew at the Ritz, where we were celebrating. He stared for a minute and then wrote a note with his phone. When I asked, he said it was nothing."

"We haven't been able to get into his phone messages yet. But I'll see if we can identify a note he may have made. He said nothing about who he saw?"

"I asked him a couple of times. I was teasing him because he seemed so intense, and I wanted this to be a fun time. Do you think this has something to do with your case?" Jerome now looked over to see how Mae was handling all of this.

"I hope whoever did this to Marko ends up in the river!" Mae was not holding back her feelings. "He was an angel. Whenever I needed something, and Jerome was busy, I could always call Marko. He was like a son to me. I miss him so much." Mae brought an embroidered handkerchief to her eyes.

"I miss him, too," Alan quietly said. "We will find out who did this and there will be justice. In the meantime, I don't know if you're aware of this, but Marko has a brother who lives in Boston. Would you like to meet him?"

Mae and Jerome looked surprised. There was more of Marko's life to learn.

"Yes!" They both stated at once. Alan gave them Sidney's name and promised to relate this to him.

As Alan drove away from the visit, he had mixed emotions. Jerome and Mae were gentle caring friends, the types he now expected Marko to have. But why didn't he tell his friends he had a brother living in Boston? Alan understood that humans were not perfect and sometimes a person's past drives their motivation. Isn't that what Rose was trying to get him to understand?

It took Alan over a half hour in traffic to get through the city. Traffic in Boston had to be the worst in the country, although he'd read that Seattle had them beat. As he sat in traffic, he considered how the road map to relationships seemed overwhelming at his age. Being single offered independence, but his lack of connections with others could mean a lonely existence in the end.

Alan wondered who his real friends were. He thought about Enrique, but Alan was much older and didn't really have a lot in common with him except for work. In fact, he was probably Enrique's father's age. Once again, he acknowledged his limitations. Now that retirement was looming even closer, what was he planning for the next stage of his life? Maybe he should consider moving to the West Coast to be closer to his daughter and grandchildren.

With that thought in mind, Alan walked into the condo and found Sam asleep on the couch. Harry ran up and barked a greeting to Alan, causing Sam to awaken. "Hey, how was your day?" Alan asked

"Good, what time is it?" Sam slowly sat up and shook his head. "Did you eat yet?"

Alan smiled, because that was exactly what he was going to ask. "Chinese?"

"Sounds good. Do you want to have it delivered or can I go get it?"

Alan looked attentively at his blinking son. Obviously, he had been deep in sleep. "I'll order it delivered."

Walking to his room to change into comfortable garb, Alan wondered if it was the right time to ask Sam about the pills he found in his room. There was the nagging yearning to be more transparent with Sam and treat him as an adult. He didn't want to pressure him, but Alan thought he would try to open the conversation and remember not to advise or judge.

The food arrived faster than expected. After all, this was Monday and most people had eaten enough take out over the weekend Alan guessed. While attacking the fried rice with chop sticks, Alan asked about Sam's day at work again.

"I'm taking the online classes on research grants all morning this week. They're a huge help with organizing my thoughts and creating a plan. Then in the afternoon I spend time going through files for names of contributors. There are several big donors on the list. I saw Marko's name on some of them as a contact." Sam looked warily at his father, hoping he'd not divulged something confidential.

"Really? That may be something I need to investigate. I hadn't thought about Marko's involvement with that part of the center. Of course, he must have spread the word about the work they were doing. Thanks for telling me." Alan nodded appreciatively at his son. "Did you talk with Maryanne today?"

"No," Sam seemed disappointed, rubbing at the back of his neck. "I guess I'll give her some space. She separated from her ex only ten months ago and doesn't want to get into a relationship right off the bat. She's also saving to move back to the West Coast in a year. She misses her family."

"Speaking of family," Alan responded, "When was the last time you spoke with your sister? I try to call her on Sundays, but lately I've dropped the ball."

"I hardly ever talk with her. She's busy with her kids and job anyway. When I thought about moving in with someone, I never considered her or mom. They both want to take over my life and give advice that I just don't want to hear." Alan gave Sam a look of understanding. "I totally understand, son. They mean well, but we guys can figure things out ourselves. Even if we make mistakes and mess up along the way."

Alan gave this a minute to sink in and then decided to ask Sam about the pills. "Sam, I was looking for Harry's leash today to take him for a short walk. I found it in your room and noticed a bottle of pills on the nightstand. Do you want to talk about this?"

Sam looked quickly up from his plate of food. "Were you going through my stuff?"

"No, the leash was right by your bed and the pills were obviously in sight. Why are you taking them?"

Sam took his time to respond, sitting back from the table and folding his arms across his chest. "I was given a prescription of Adderall when I was in college because I was having a difficult time keeping up with my studies." Sam stood up and began to pace the room. "Once I started taking the pills, everything got easier. Not only with my studies, but also socially. I felt on top of my game and my entire life and thought I was moving forward for the first time. You know?" He sat back down in the chair and put his head in his hands.

Alan nodded. "But why continue to take it now?"

"I'm trying to stop. But I must've developed some sort of physical dependence because when I start to taper off, I get headaches and feel sick, like I have the flu." Sam looked defeated.

"How can I help?" Alan put his hand on Sam's shoulder to reassure him that he wasn't judging, only offering help.

"Well, I guess I do need help. I've spent time looking up information on this drug. Nothing is straight forward, largely because of the stigma and shame associated with addiction." Sam lowered his head. "I'm not sure what to do... maybe go to a clinic or even rehab. I heard they have outpatients now."

"Let's take it a step at a time. Carla would be the person to ask, but I'm sure you don't want to go that route." Sam shook his head. "I'll ask one of the narcotics officers that I trust at the precinct what they would recommend. Then it will be up to you. I'll always be here for you, but it's your journey."

Sam let out a little sigh of relief. "Thanks, Dad. I really feel embarrassed and guilty having you find out about this. I figured I could handle it on my own, but your support will really help."

Alan gave Sam a thumbs up. "Let me know what you need."

Just as Sam turned to leave the kitchen, Alan had another idea. "You might be able to help me with something. I just learned that Marko was getting a team of his kids together for basketball at a gym near the teen center. How would you like to go and see if you could help? It might give you an opportunity to meet some of the kids in the program."

Sam looked enthused. "Sure. I'm not a great

basketball player, but I love the game."

Alan was pleased with Sam's desire to get involved. He didn't even take the time to deliberate the decision, it seemed to come at the same moment as the idea.

# TUESDAY, MAY 24<sup>TH</sup>

Enrique was uncomfortable making an appointment to talk with David Reagan. In his mind all realtors seemed to be like used car salesmen, promising something they could never deliver. He and Marie had bought their home after months of haggling with two representatives who just wanted to make money. The good news was that they loved their house and promised each other they would never sell it, mainly to avoid this type of harassment again.

Walking into the opulent building that Alan had described so perfectly, Enrique gave his card to the young receptionist. Her perfect make-up, long eyelashes and mauve lipstick reminded him of the young singers on MTV he used to watch when he was a kid. Do things never change? She picked up the phone with her lacquered nails and rang her boss.

David Reagan opened his door a few minutes later and thrust his hand out. "Good morning, Detective, please come in. Would you like some tea or coffee?"

Enrique accepted the offer of coffee and Reagan nodded to the young receptionist. Entering the sophisticated office, Enrique took a chair near Reagan's expensive desk. He refused to be intimidated, but it would be an effort. "I understand that Detective Sharp has already asked you questions about the building that was destroyed. I just need to clarify a couple more things."

Reagan shifted his bulky weight in his over-sized chair and stared directly at Enrique. "What do you need to know?"

"You seem to have several companies that service that building. We're wondering who you work with directly. Who fixes the problems for you when something goes wrong?" Enrique gave an innocent look to Reagan, trying to appear as if this question was expected.

"Well, I usually have my assistant handle all the problems. He manages my buildings and lets me know when something goes wrong. He also works part-time for city utilities and is familiar with power and sewage structure in the buildings, piping and wiring and that sort of thing. He's quite handy in making normal repairs and replacing small equipment, et cetera." Reagan sat back and seemed pleased with his answer. "Henry Olson is his name. He's been working for me part time for a couple years and can absolutely be trusted." He reached for a piece of note paper and handed over Olson's contact details.

"Thank you," Enrique put the paper in his notebook. "Can you tell me if that building was zoned for anything other than residences? We understand there are historical committees working on preserving the St. Botolph area and wonder if you've spoken with them."

"Detective, I'm still in the process of working through

the insurance details with my adjuster. Any zoning or reconstruction will be dealt with later. If there is a committee, then I will have someone meet with them. I don't know why this would be any interest to you."

Being distracted for a moment, Enrique reached for the coffee the receptionist had just brought in. He attempted to look through his notes for a second time and thinking out loud, Enrique quietly said, "It just seems that someone might benefit from damaging this old building and making some money on the location." He glanced up at Reagan.

"I will keep that in mind. If that's all you want to know, please understand that I have another client I need to see." Reagan stood up and offered his hand.

"One more question, did you know the deceased, Marko Miller?"

Reagan continued to stand and looked defensively at Enrique. "No. I have never met the man. I have no idea what he was doing in my building, and I am very sorry he died there."

It took Enrique three tries to get his notebook into his coat pocket. He looked warily at the coffee mug, placed it back on Reagan's desk and shook his hand. "I'll let you know if we have more questions." Walking past the receptionist, he noticed her nails were a deep maroon which matched the carpet. He shook his head and smiled slightly.

Hearing the name of Henry Olson again was probably a good lead. Enrique called Alan and gave him an update on his conversation with Reagan.

Alan listened and decided, "We have to get ahold of

this Olson today. Will you try his number?"

Enrique dialed the business phone for Olson and got voicemail. He left a message saying that he and Alan would like to talk with him. He then called the office number to see if Olson was working today. He was. Enrique called Alan back. "The utility company says Olson gets in today at noon. Why don't we pay him a visit?"

Alan agreed they should try and track down Olson before Reagan got to him, although it might be too late already. Alan looked at his watch. He had an hour to finish with his calls and make it in time to meet Enrique. "I'll meet you there."

Henry Olson was worried. And when he got this worried his anger flared. Someone at the police department wanted to speak with him about the fire on St. Botolph Street. He had to call Reagan and find out what he told them if anything. Reaching for his phone, he dialed Reagan's private line.

"Reagan."

"Hey, this is Olson. The police just called to talk about the fire. What'd you tell them?"

"Nothing. I was out of town anyway."

"That's great…you've got an alibi. What about me?"

"It's up to you. Lie if you must…make something up. I don't care. Just be certain they believe you were nowhere around when it happened."

Olson's anger burst forth, "I'm not going to go down for this!"

Alan and Enrique had been given a description of Olson and were waiting by the truck loading zone when his pickup drove in. As he got out of his car and noticed the pair, obviously cops, he looked cautiously around. Was he going to run, thought Alan? Taking out his shield and walking to meet him, the officers approached quickly.

"Mr. Olson, we'd like to ask you a few questions." Alan looked determined. "Do you have some place we could talk around here?"

Olson looking upset, motioned to the office building which appeared to be empty. Inside was a table with four chairs where the three men convened. "What's your connection with the house on St. Botolph Street that burned on Saturday night?"

"I manage the building for David Reagan." Olson stared at both men, trying not to give in to his anxiety.

"What do you do, managing?" Alan asked.

Olson quickly recited his duties. "I collect the rent and keep an eye on the place, small repairs. That's about it."

"We know you also read the meters, right?" Enrique looked at his notes to confirm this.

"Yeah, it's part of my territory."

"How often do you usually go to the building?"

"Whenever I need to." At this point Olson was getting irritated. "Why are you asking me these questions?"

Alan calmly leaned forward and spoke firmly, "Mr. Olson, a murder was committed at that location, and we need to follow up with anyone who has access to the building. In fact, we're having a difficult time getting a hold of the tenants who live there. Do you know how to reach them?"

Olson deferred, "David Reagan keeps all that information. You have to ask him."

Alan smiled. He expected this answer. "Didn't you have to let the tenants know to leave for the weekend because of the exterminator fumigating that weekend?"

Olson began rubbing his hands on his legs, a nervous gesture which both officers noticed. "I sent them a flier."

"When were they supposed to return?" Enrique was still writing notes and appeared interested in this answer.

"Sunday evening." Olson was not giving any extra information. He sat with his arms folded and seemed to be holding on to some anger. Alan didn't want to press him, so he quietly continued.

"Speaking of the exterminators, what company did you use?"

Olson thought for a minute, his eyes darting back and forth. "It's a private company outside the city. I have all their information at my house."

"We need to know the name. Were you there when they set up?"

"No, actually. I left a key for them and said I would lock up later."

"So, you didn't talk with them that day?"

"No."

"Have you spoken to them since then?"

"No."

"So, you don't even know if they did the job." Alan was beginning to get skeptical. It didn't seem a very good policy to let someone into a building without supervision.

Olson just sat there. He looked like he was finished answering questions. Enrique noticed his tense body language and knew he was lying or not telling them something.

Alan seemed to agree. "Okay, Mr. Olson. Thank you for your time. We'll be in touch. Please remember to send us the name of that company." He put his card on the table in front of Olsen.

As they walked out the door, they noticed Olson reaching for his phone. Was he calling Reagan?

When the police left, Olson knew he was in jeopardy. He had been hung out to dry by Reagan and now his anger was building. It was just his luck that Reagan had come up with the plan to set the fire. It was supposed to be an easy way to make money. The idiot hadn't even given him the money he was owed. Now what?

Olson had suspected the black guy from the teen center had been watching him all along. He kept showing up at that building and snooping around. He seemed to be friends with the old lady on the first floor, but Olson was suspicious and wondered if he was really an undercover cop. He was also worried that Eddie Pearson had been squealing and told this guy who his dealer was. Well, it was time to protect himself. He would quit Reagan and quit the Utility Company at the same time. He had a tidy business dealing drugs and soon he would have enough money to retire.

Olson's money was safely hidden in a safe deposit box and would be enough to keep him flush. When things died down and if he played his cards right, he was on the verge of getting more clients from the lady dealer on St. Botolph Street. She worked in the city and had upscale clients who demanded expensive drugs. And if he was smart, and very careful, maybe he would sell most of his current distribution network to one of the kids, like a franchise. But right now, Olson had to think fast.

Too many things were coming down at once. He realized that if the police were nosing around, they might find out his drug connections to that building. Not to mention his part in the fire and what went down that night. He was feeling increasingly anxious and needed time to think, so he called his boss at the utility company and said he was taking the next few days off. His brother in Albany would let him wait there until he decided what to do.

Alan had another lead on his mind. Who was the person, or persons, Marko noticed that night when he and Jerome were celebrating at the Ritz? Did the restaurant have security cameras? Alan decided to stop and speak with the manager.

The Ritz Carleton was in the heart of Boston on Avery Street directly across from the Boston Common. This beautifully maintained and well-known park delivered expansive views from the 193 guest rooms and suites at the Ritz. If you had to ask the price of a room, you probably couldn't afford to stay. Within the Hotel, there were two dining spaces as well as the exclusive Equinox Sports Club for members only. One dining area, the Avery Bar, was designed to welcome guests with warm paneling and leather bench seats which inspired patrons to settle in and indulge. The menu offered the famous signature martinis along with a variety of starters and small entrees. Catering to the wealthy, sophisticated, and social elite of Boston, the other dining room was the Artisan Bistro with its lofty ambience and offer of a full menu. This restaurant was always popular with the locals on weekends for their famous lobster crepes.

Alan walked into the elegant wood paneled lobby of the Ritz. The old-world design on the carpeting and dim lighting from wall sconces provided a warmth and added a somewhat dramatic feeling of old-world hospitality. He stopped and took in his bearings. Approaching him was a young gentleman wearing what looked like a tuxedo or a morning suit inquiring if he might help Alan. The shining brass name pin he wore introduced him as Harold. He was scrutinizing Alan carefully, studying his clothes and probably adding up the cost. Alan shopped at Men's Warehouse and was amused with the apparent judgement being made. At least he had worn a tie.

"I'm here to speak with the manager," Alan pulled out his ID and stared at Harold. He couldn't be more than 25 and was probably the son of some board member in the city. Boston was famous for nepotism.

"Let me make a phone call, sir." Harold escorted Alan to a saddle grey leather chair with bronze fasteners. It was surprisingly comfortable. "May I get you some coffee or tea?" Harold was now very attentive and seemed to linger longer than necessary.

"After you've made the phone call to the manager, yes, I would like some coffee." Alan wanted Harold to know he was here on business and not for a casual meeting.

Harold returned minutes later holding a tray of coffee with sugar and cream and asked Alan to follow him. He led him to a small, yet luxurious, office of the hotel manager. After shaking hands with a rather elegant older man, Alan was offered another very comfortable leather chair. Before taking a sip of his coffee, Alan stated his business. "I'm investigating the murder of someone who had drinks at your bar on the Friday before last."

"Well," interrupted the manager, "I'm sorry to hear someone has died, but I don't keep track of my patrons. How would I know who he or she is?"

Smiling, Alan began again. "The man who was murdered happened to see someone he knew having dinner that night. I was hoping you had receipts from your patrons, so I could try and find out who he or she might be. It was between ten and eleven." Alan waited for the manager to say the obvious.

"Do you have a court order or a warrant to search through my receipts? We are a very discreet establishment, and do not give out names of people who dine or stay with us. This would go against all our privacy assurances to our customers."

"I understand your concern. Perhaps it would be easier if we saw the recordings from the security cameras from outside the building. Anyone leaving the hotel between ten and closing would greatly help us. Or we could also interview the servers who were here that evening, I'm sure I could gather a team of uniformed officers to come down and talk with them, maybe in the lobby." Alan brought out his notebook and prepared to write down names.

"Okay, let me make a phone call." Grabbing the phone on his desk and twisting around to the window, the manager quietly spoke to someone in security. It was arranged for Alan to look through the camera footage of that night, but he would not be able to speak with the servers.

Alan placed his coffee cup back on the tray and thanked the manager. Harold arrived seconds later and led him to the security room.

In truth, Alan had no idea who he was looking for. Marko's life was beginning to be a puzzle and anyone he might have seen that night might be unknown to him. Looking though the video brought no surprises, but he requested a copy anyway. He would show it to Carla and Jerome and see if they had a clue.

On the way back to the office, Alan called Sarah in Tech services to see if she found anything on Marko's phone.

"Well, there were a few messages that didn't make any sense. I'll copy and send them right now." Sarah seemed perplexed with her findings.

"Look on his notes app and see if there's something from that Friday night," Alan had no clue what a notes app was, but it sounded like the right thing. He wished he knew more about all the various apps and programs and doodads these contraptions offered. Even if he learned something new today, it would probably change tomorrow. At least that's what he'd heard.

"Okay, I did find a note from that night. Do you want me to read it to you?"

"Sure. And copy and send it too."

"It says, 'ask EP about SB deal'. That's it."

"Thank you, Sarah. If you see anything else of interest, just forward it to me."

Before returning to the office, Alan drove to the teen center to talk with Carla. She was in a meeting when he arrived, so he thought he'd see if Sam was free. Asking a few people for directions, Alan found Sam in the computer room with earphones on, seeming to be entertained with something online. When he saw his father, Sam clicked off the program and stood up. "What are you doing here?"

Alan shrugged, "I need to speak with Carla, but she's with someone. I thought I would say hi to you as long as I'm here. It looks like you're busy, so I'll see you later at home." He began to turn around when Sam said, "Wait. Do you want a cup of coffee? I can take a break now." Although it seemed awkward for them both, they decided a quick cup of coffee would be a good idea.

"What were you working on when I saw you? You seemed to be enjoying it." Alan hoped he wasn't intruding on Sam's work and felt his shoulders tense up as he waited for a reply.

"Oh, it was a funny article I had to read about grants. Some people apply for the weirdest things! This one family wanted money to send their five-year-old to art school. They were convinced she was the next O'Keefe. And another family wanted money for their twenty-nine-year-old son to start a business because they were so tired of him living with them at home. There's a list of all sorts of crazy things people ask for." Alan loved watching how animated Sam was while sharing this information.

"Yep, in my experience, people are always trying to get around the rules." Alan shook his head slightly and then looked around when he heard Carla's voice.

"Alan! I was just going to call you. How are you doing, Sam, is the class still intriguing?"

Sam stood up quickly and said, "It's going great. I better get back to it."

Carla and Alan returned to her office and shut the door. Carla nervously began, "I've heard some interesting stories about St Botolph Street that might interest you. It appears Marko knew about a drug dealer who sold from that one building. This dealer had been approaching some of the teens and warning them they were being followed and that it was probably an undercover cop. I hate to think this, but what if one of them identified Marko as working with the police? You and he worked so closely on cases... could that have raised suspicions?"

Alan absorbed this new information for a moment, "Hmmm... that might explain some things. I'll need to think about it."

"Meanwhile, there's something else you can help me with," Alan took the security CD out of his pocket and looked around for a computer. "We'll have to go to the computer room, because it looks like you only have your laptop here."

Using the computer facing the far wall, Carla and Alan

scanned the Ritz hotel recording as people walked to their cars. Not recognizing anyone, the CD was almost over when Carla saw something. "Go back! I know who that couple might be." Slowly retracing the film, Carla had Alan stop for a man and woman who appeared to be hurrying down the few steps. "I think that's Eddie's parents. It would make sense because they're one of the wealthier families whose son is connected to the center. Why is this important?"

"Jerome and Marko were having drinks together at the Ritz on the Friday before he died. While there, Jerome said Marko seemed upset because he saw someone he knew. He wrote something on his phone app, and it read, 'ask EP about SB deal'."

Carla raised her eyebrows and said, "Eddie Pearson about St. Botolph? Do you think this family is involved with drugs?"

"It's an idea. And right now, we're looking into everything. When I tried to interview Eddie he walked away, so it's time I called him into the precinct and find out what he's hiding. My guess is that his father will come along, too." Alan took the CD out of the computer and stood up. "Let's keep this between us, of course." Carla understood.

It was already 1:00 and Alan was starving so he stopped for two chicken sandwiches and chips for himself and Enrique. The first thing he did when he got back to the office was to call Eddie Pearson to come in for an interview. He left a voicemail.

Enrique hurried into the office to find Alan just finishing his sandwich. Grabbing the lunch sack Alan had bought for him, he quickly sat at his desk and gathered his notes.

"Go ahead and eat your lunch while I tell you about what I found out today." Alan walked to the incident board and pointed to Eddie Pearson's name. "This kid is the one who didn't want to talk with me when I met him at school. He definitely has an attitude and thinks he's a smart guy. When I went to the Ritz today, the security guy gave me a video of the people who left the restaurant on the Friday night when Jerome and Marko were there. I didn't know anyone who appeared on the film, but when I took it to Carla, she identified the Pearson's. To top it off, Sarah, in computers, says that the note Marko made to himself that Friday night says, 'ask EP about SB deal.' That could very well mean that Marko was getting closer to knowing who was dealing to teens at that building."

Enrique stopped eating, "Did you call Eddie in to talk?"

"I just left him a voicemail. We need to be careful because they might lawyer up quickly before we find out what Eddie knows."

Alan pointed to the incident board once more. "We've got the Pearsons and Henry Olson who works for David Reagan to focus on now. Let's assume we're working on two different crimes, the arson, and the murder. If Reagan wanted to damage the building in order to rebuild on the site, then arson would be a tidy way to go. It's what you call a crime of opportunity, any moron can start a fire and never get caught. But the murder may involve drugs and Marko might have been at the wrong place at the wrong time."

"Did you get any leads on the vehicles from the list the guy on St. Botolph Street gave you?"

Enrique searched his phone to see if the DMV tech had found anything. "Nothing yet. But it looks like the Utility Company pickup truck makes quite a few trips in that neighborhood. That puts Olson on site and provides an opportunity for him to deal if he wanted to."

Enrique stood up and pointed to Henry Olson's name. "What if Marko just happened to be entering the building when Olson was starting the fire? Or maybe Marko was already dead when Olson entered the building and he panicked and got the job done and then disappeared."

Alan looked up in agreement. "That might be exactly what happened. Someone knew the building was empty and arranged to meet Marko there sometime on Saturday. Let's go with this thought while we interview Pearson. But first I want you to take a picture of Eddie to Trudy and see if this is the same teenager she saw Marko arguing with on the street."

Enrique grimaced, "That lady drives me crazy. She's obnoxious! You owe me one."

When Alan still hadn't heard from Eddie Pearson, he sent two police officers to the High School to find him. Although the Principal was alarmed, he called for Eddie to come to the office. At the same time, he called Mr. Pearson to let him know what was happening. When Eddie stomped into the school office, he was stunned to see the police waiting for him.

"What do you want me for?" Eddie looked irritated

and on the verge of running. One officer took his arm and led him to the patrol car. On the way he told Eddie that he was needed for some questioning.

E nrique pushed on the intercom bell to Trudy's apartment, almost hoping she wasn't home. When she answered, she was annoyed to hear the detective's voice. She didn't want to get more involved with this investigation and showed her displeasure when she opened her door. With her arms crossed she glared at him. He held up his hand, "Just one question, please. Do you know this kid?" Enrique showed Trudy Eddie's school photo. Grabbing the photo to show her impatience, Trudy stared at the photo. "I don't know his name, but I've seen him around here. He dresses weirdly, I remember that." She had already lied to the other detective about seeing Marko with some kid, and she didn't want to get further into her lie.

"Is he the one you saw Marko arguing with?"

Trudy hesitated, "I'm not certain. All the kids hanging around here are strange and I try my best to ignore them." This was an exaggeration, of course, but maybe the police would finally leave her alone.

Without pausing to say goodbye, Enrique hurried down the steps and called Alan from his car. "She couldn't make an ID. But she's sure lying about something. Do you want me to do anything else, or come back to the precinct?" Alan wanted him to return and help interview Eddie Pearson.

Eddie was scared but tried to maintain a sullen stance as he was led into an interview room. He had been in trouble before on minor offenses, and his father always got him out of being charged. He was certain his father's lawyer would be called, and this would be over in no time.

Alan let Eddie sit in the room alone until Enrique returned. He also expected Mr. Pearson to show up, probably with his attorney. True to form, twenty minutes later a very irritated and loud person entered the office demanding to speak with his son. Alan asked him to sit while he appeared to be organizing some notes. He was aware that Pearson was looking at the incident board and could see his son's name on it.

"What's going on here? Why's my son's name on this board? I want answers now or I'll call my attorney and you will hear about it from people in charge of this place!" His reddened face was bursting with anger and Alan hoped he would calm down.

Alan looked up from his paperwork and said, "Mr. Pearson, I tried to interview your son at his school last week and he refused to answer my questions. Now we have some new information and decided to bring him into the precinct to see if he will cooperate. You have a right to be with him if he chooses, but because he's eighteen, we can question him alone as an adult." Alan was direct and firm. He disliked this man and knew his son probably did too.

"I want to talk with Eddie first," demanded Pearson.

"I have a right to advise him after I know what you are questioning him about."

"We are investigating a murder, Mr. Pearson, and your son knew the victim and was seen talking with him shortly before he was found dead. The victim's name was Marko Miller and if you know him and could be of assistance then please tell us. Otherwise, I need to interview your son." Alan picked up some notes on his desk and moved to the door, leaving Pearson with his anger and on the phone to his attorney.

Eddie was pacing the floor when Alan entered the room. To worry Eddie even more, Alan turned on a tape recorder and gave his name and the time and the reason for the interview. Eddie slammed down his fist on the table, "Why am I here?"

"You apparently didn't want to talk with me at your school last week and I informed you at the time I would have you brought in for a talk."

Enrique entered the room at this point and sat next to Alan. He looked sternly at Eddie, letting him know how serious this might be.

Alan took out a picture of Marko from his file and asked, "Do you know this man?"

"Of course, I do! You already know that!"

"Please tell us his name and how you know him," Alan maintained a steady voice.

Giving a long sigh, Eddie muttered, "It's Marko Miller. He works at the teen center, and I knew him there."

"Did you have any other contact with Marko other

than the center?"

"No."

"We have a witness who saw you arguing with him the week before he was killed. Do you remember this argument?"

Eddie squirmed in his chair and rubbed his hand over his eyes. "Do I need a lawyer?"

"It's up to you. It would help us if you could just answer a few questions about your relationship with Marko. By the way, your father is outside in the office. The school Principal called him when you left the building. Would you like him to join us?"

Eddie looked up to see Enrique still staring at him. "No, I do not want to talk with my father."

"When was the last time you saw Marko?"

Eddie's eyes scanned the room, either trying to remember, or deciding to lie. "I saw him at the center, probably the week before that fire."

"Did you talk with him at any time on Saturday, May 15th? We have reason to believe that he wanted to get in touch with you that day."

"I can't remember." Eddie laid his head in his folded hands on the table.

Alan and Enrique both left the room. They needed to discuss their options because they had no proof that Eddie was involved with Marko's death and knew they couldn't keep him. Enrique noted that if they let him go, they could watch him carefully and see where he goes and who he contacts. Alan reluctantly agreed to this plan. He opened the door and told Eddie they were done.

"We might want to talk with you later." Alan said sternly as he stepped aside, holding back the disgust he felt for this kid. He watched as Eddie peered around the office, hoping to avoid his father whose back was turned to him. Retreating out the main door in a hurry, Eddie looked like a scared rabbit. Alan walked over to Mr. Pearson and told him they had let his son go with a warning, but he may be called in again for more questioning.

"You will be hearing from my lawyer if you do!" Pearson stomped out the door, reminding Alan of the same belligerent attitude he saw in Eddie.

*Something was wrong*, Alan thought. Who was Eddie Pearson really upset with? Maybe it was some drug dealer who was refusing to go along with his schemes or his story. So far, there was nothing to connect him to the crime, but why does he act so guilty? Alan's intuition was buzzing. Somehow, he suspected, Eddie was involved with Marko's death.

Alan looked at the time and told Enrique to go home and enjoy his family. They would meet again in the morning to review and make decisions. Alan had another stop to make. He was going to talk with Tony again.

It was getting late when Alan arrived on St. Botolph Street, and Tony was just about to lock up his store. When he saw Detective Sharp approaching, he opened the door and drew the curtain on the window after letting him in. "You caught me just in time, Detective. How can I help?"

Alan got right to the point, as usual. Taking out a photo of Eddie Pearson, he asked Tony if he recognized him.

"Yes, in fact that's the kid Marko wanted me to keep an eye on. He was either a dealer or just a druggy, but Marko was very concerned for his welfare."

"Do you know if he dealt drugs?"

"I suspected he did, but only to his pals at school. He seems like an insecure kid who's all bravado and no spine. Isn't his father some kind of investor or something?"

Alan nodded, "Something like that, I guess. Did Marko say anything else about Eddie? Did he hang around here often? Did he meet with people who looked shady?" Alan realized these questions were vague and he was just thinking out loud. He paused and looked at Tony for any information he could help with.

"I wish I'd paid more attention. It was only recently that Marko asked me to keep a lookout for this kid. When I saw the kid, he was always by himself, just hanging around. If he had anything to do with that old building, I didn't know about it. Have you heard from any of the tenants from that address yet? The only one I know who lived there for several years is old. She's having some health problems and her family's been looking in on her occasionally. I've got the family's number here somewhere." Tony went behind his counter and opened a drawer of notes. Riffling through them, he finally found the information. "Her name was Briggs, Patricia Briggs. A real nice lady. This is her family's address and phone number."

Alan took the information down and thanked Tony. "If you think of anything else about Eddie Pearson or drug activity on the street, be sure to call me. Thanks again Tony, this has been a great help."

It was only 6:30 and so Alan decided to call the number Tony gave him and find out if Patricia Briggs was with her family. Sometimes he had the good luck to come across a witness who was both honest and direct. Because she was old, he hoped that Miss Briggs would be such a witness.

Patricia and her family were just finishing dinner when the call came. Her daughter, Doreen, answered the call and looked perplexed. "That was a detective calling for you, Mom. He wants to ask you some questions about your apartment. They're probably talking with the residents because of the fire. I hope it's okay with you, he's coming by in half an hour."

Patricia got a tear in her eye. "Fine with me," she put her fork down on her plate and thought for a minute. "You know, I'd love to help find whoever set fire to my building. All of my old things are gone and all of my memories with them." She took out a handkerchief and dabbed her eyes. At eighty, her tears came more often than she planned.

When Alan rang the doorbell, he was surprised to see the older lady opening the door and holding out her hand. "Glad to meet you Detective," she greeted, "Come in and have a cup of tea with me." Dressed in a lavender velour sweatsuit and very white sneakers, Patricia led the way into a comfortable living room. Tea and cookies were already laid out on the coffee table and Patricia began to pour. "Now, tell me, how can I help you?"

Totally charmed with this lady, Alan smiled and gently began his inquiries. "I'm wondering how long you lived in your apartment on St. Botolph Street." Patricia looked intently at

Alan and said, "I've been there for over thirty years. It's not, or wasn't, a large apartment, but it had everything I needed, including a bedroom and a quilt room. It was only six hundred square feet, Detective, but it was perfect." Patricia took a sip of tea and hoped her emotions wouldn't overcome her.

"You must have seen a lot of different tenants come and go over the years. I'm wondering if you ever saw this man in your building." Alan showed her Marko's photo.

"Yes! That's my friend Marko! I haven't seen him since the fire. Are you here because of him?" Patricia now looked fearful, hoping her friend was okay.

Alan slowly reached out to hold Patricia's hand. "I'm afraid that Marko died in the fire. I'm sorry to have to tell you this sad news." He looked around to hear if someone else was in the house in case she needed some added support. Patricia let out a hard sigh and closed her eyes. With a pained expression, she asked, "Who did this?"

"We're investigating every possibility. Are you feeling okay to answer just a few questions?"

Making no attempt to wipe away her tears, Patricia agreed to help. Alan began, "How did you get to know Marko?"

"Well, let's see, it was about two years ago, I guess. He was standing outside of the building when I was coming back from my walk to the corner store. I asked him if I could help him with something and he gave me the nicest smile. He said he was supposed to meet someone at this address and the person hadn't shown up yet. I asked him if he wanted to wait inside, but he said no. It was just so like Marko, never wanting to put anyone out."

"So, you got to know him better somehow?"

"Yes! He started coming around every so often to meet someone, although I never found out who that person was as a matter of fact. I never thought it was my business. Anyway, I started asking him in for tea every time I saw him. He was an excellent listener. And he told me all about his job at the teen center and the drag dresses, too." At this point she smiled broadly. "I loved the stories about the drag queens."

"Did Marko ever mention something that he was worried about? Or someone he was watching?"

"Like I said, Marko let me talk while he listened. The last time I saw him was when we were all told to leave the building for the weekend so they could exterminate the rats and bugs. Marko came by on Friday afternoon to make sure I had a ride to my daughter's house. He was like that, so caring. Anyway, my daughter was picking me up, so I didn't need a ride."

"Patricia, we have information there were drugs being sold around and inside your building. Do you know anything about that?"

"I always suspected it. I would speak with the patrol officers whenever I saw them and let them know what I suspected. Sometimes there were loud parties in the upstairs apartments, and I had to take my hearing aids out so I could get some sleep. It seemed that people moved out and new people moved in quite a lot. I never really got to know anyone."

Alan took another photo out of his notebook and showed to Patricia. "Have you seen this teenager around?"

Patricia took the photo from Alan and studied it. She then took her reading glasses out of her velour jacket pocket and frowned at the photo. "I think I've seen him hanging around. I think he's the one that wears strange clothes and walks with an attitude." She looked up to see if Alan agreed with her.

"His name is Eddie Pearson, and he may be in the middle of something. We're keeping an eye on him." Alan took the photo and continued, "Who do you pay your utility bill to? Is it Boston Utility Company?

"Oh no, we just get charged for all utilities in our rent. When the rent goes up, we get a notice that the electricity and water have increased their costs. It's frustrating because it may happen more than once a year." Alan raised his eyebrows with this news. There was rent control in the city and owners were not allowed to raise rent more than once a year. He would check on this.

"What will you do now? I imagine you have lost most of your possessions in the fire." Alan tilted his head in concern for this elderly woman.

"My daughter wants me to move in here. I guess it's time for me to give up some of my independence and realize I may be getting on in years. I feel younger than I look." Patricia smiled sweetly at Alan, probably hoping he would understand. He winked.

"Thank you for your help, Patricia. I'm sorry to bring you such sad news. If there is a memorial service, I'll be sure and let you know." Alan stood and offered his hand to Patricia.

"Detective, do you have a card? Just in case I think of anything else." She smiled again, hoping he would give her his card. She wanted to show her grandchildren. Alan reached in his pocket and handed his card to her. "Please call me anytime."

It had been a long day, and Alan needed to get home. He wondered if he should call Sam and pick up something for dinner. Would this become a habit? They still haven't figured out a plan for living side by side. He decided to just drive home.

Harry ran to the door when Alan arrived. In the kitchen, Sam was busy making something that smelled pretty good. "Hey dad," he called out, "I've got some pasta cooking. Are you hungry?"

"Yes!" Alan followed the aroma of garlic into the kitchen. "It smells terrific!" He looked at the open bottle of red wine on the counter and poured himself a glass. "You know, I could get used to having a chef, "Alan kidded. "But please let me buy the groceries from now on. You shouldn't have to spend your money like this."

"You're letting me stay here, it's the least I can do. I'll let you know if I come up short, okay?"

Alan and Sam both nodded in unison. It was true, Sam didn't pay rent and Alan would never ask him to. If he saved his money, they both knew he would eventually find a place of his own.

"I met Sidney Miller today," Sam said. "He seems like

a really nice guy."

"You did? Where did you meet him?" Alan was surprised and curious about this.

"He came in to talk with Carla. She introduced me to him because he wants to volunteer at the center. I guess his attorney skills would always be appreciated, and he said he could help me with some of the grant writing. The legal part, you know."

"That's wonderful! My gosh, things are changing and moving quickly. I was going to call Sidney tomorrow. I try and keep him up to date on the case. I'm happy to hear he's lent his skills to the center." Alan dished up a huge plate of pasta, three pieces of hot garlic bread and a small salad. He didn't realize how hungry he was until he sat down.

When dinner was over and Alan finished washing the dishes, he asked Sam if he had seen Maryanne lately. "I called her a couple of times," Sam said, "But she was busy. I know she doesn't want to get involved with anyone, but I was hoping we could just hang out." Sam looked disappointed and flopped on the sofa and turned on the TV. "Do you want to watch something?"

Looking at his watch, Alan realized he had enough time to make the last show at the Dragonfly where Jerome was performing. "Sam, I want to go see one of the shows at the drag theater where Marko Miller worked. There are a few people I need to talk with who knew Marko and this could be my opportunity. Do you by any chance want to tag along?"

"Sure!" Sam jumped up off the sofa and went to get his jacket.

The theater was not difficult to find because of the colorfully dressed theatre-goers who were waiting in line. Dressed in his usual black slacks and white shirt, Alan felt drab and out of place. Sam, on the other hand, was wearing his typical cargo shorts and a pink shirt that read something about pink being a man's color. He also had on a Bruins hat and jacket that made him look younger than his twenty-four years. Alan noted that he seemed to be enjoying the crowd.

Stepping in line for tickets, Sam started talking with the person in line ahead of them. Not certain if this was male or female, Alan stood mute while listening to his overly curious son ask the person what the show was tonight. Dressed in a sequin bodysuit and wearing glitter makeup, the person answered with a toss of his/her wig, that it was audition night. Many of the people in line were going to perform their show numbers for the staff and hope to be given a few minutes on stage. Sam wished the person, male or female, luck and said he would root for him/her.

After purchasing tickets, Alan and Sam were escorted into the aged theater and told to find a seat. The theater was charming, gilt molding ran throughout the ceiling and walls highlighting carvings of theater symbols. On the stage, a glass chandelier dominated the set and gave an elegant appearance to what might have been an ordinary room. In contrast, strobe lights were dancing around from above and radiating onto sheer curtains that hung from the ceiling.

Looking around at the crowd, they noticed a few

empty seats in the second row on the left-hand side. Making their way to the seats, Alan noticed a couple who seemed out of place amidst the bright colors and adornment. Looking again, he saw that it was Sidney and Carla. At that moment, Carla also saw him and waved. She motioned for him to come over, and so Alan left Sam to secure their seats, and walked up the aisle to visit.

"What are you doing here?" Carla's eyebrows raised in an expression he knew well. Not one to beat around the bush, Carla was always direct.

"I wondered the same about you. Hi Sidney."

Sidney nonchalantly waved his fingers at Alan giving the impression that this was not the time or place to explain things.

"We decided to try and find out more about Marko, and this was a logical place. Are you on the clock? How come you brought Sam?"

Alan felt he needed to explain something, but he also knew that police business needed to be protected. "I wanted to talk with some of the people Marko knew here. I invited Sam to come with me as kind of an outing with his old dad. He was all for it."

The lights flickered and Alan returned to his seat. The hour-long show was a collection of songs and skits professionally acted by men of all shapes and sizes. Their gowns flowed with every movement and gave the illusion of women on the stage. That night's show had the glitz and glamour of old Hollywood in the performances. One performer had such elegance and melodramatic realness, that the crowd exploded when she turned up the heat with high kicks and belted out a rendition of "Happy Days." Impersonations of favorite personalities, particularly Cher and Tina Turner, also received thunderous applause.

During intermission, Alan told Sam he was going to find Jerome. Backstage, actors were partially clad in blurred lines between male and female. Many of them were without their wigs and fanning themselves so their make-up wouldn't melt. Jerome saw Alan and motioned to follow him to a small room. Dressed in a metallic jumpsuit layered with silk scarves that draped over his enormous fake bosom, Jerome seemed blasé about his outfit and glitzy makeup.

"How do you like the show?" Jerome gave Alan a pleading look, hoping the detective would have a positive review.

"I like it," Alan truthfully responded. "Amazing talent, and the set, choreography and costumes are very impressive."

Jerome let out a deep breath. "I'm so happy to hear you say this. We always wonder how straight guys react to our performances. And you, detective, are probably as straight as it gets." Jerome leaned his head back and gave out a loud laugh. "I hope you don't mind if I say that."

Alan was amused. "It's good to know how others view me. Now, Jerome, have you heard anything of interest about Marko's death?" Seeing Jerome's downturned mouth, Alan carefully continued, "Of course, I understand the grief of those who are mourning him, but maybe somebody knows something that would help this case."

Jerome shook his head, "I have had my ears to the

ground and not a single clue has popped up. Everyone here is grief stricken. Nobody knows a thing. Did you find out who Marko saw at the Ritz that night?"

"Yes, we did. It was the parents of a teen he was working with at the center."

"Could it be Eddie Pearson?"

"Yes." Alan felt this might help with some additional information. "Why did you ask that?"

"Poor Eddie was the one teen Marko worried about the most. He has such a bad attitude and cannot kick his habit. Marko saw a kinder and more intelligent side to him and went out of his way to give him way too many chances."

At this point the lights flickered and Jerome jumped up to get back on stage. "Tonight, we have auditions, and I'm one of the judges. I love these wannabes and their energy." Jerome hugged Alan and ran out the door.

Sam was talking with Sidney and Carla when Alan returned. Feeling exhausted from his long day, Alan asked Sam if he was ready to go home.

"Don't you want to stay and watch the amateur show?"

"No, thanks, I'm tired." Alan realized he didn't have the stamina for more entertainment tonight.

Carla saw Sam's disappointment, "We can give Sam a ride home if he wants to stay."

Sam looked hopefully at his father and then realized how exhausted he appeared. "No, thanks, I think I'll go now too. I've got work in the morning." Sam smiled at Carla.

Alan needed to sleep, even if it was for only half the

night. He tried to quit counting how many hours of sleep he got each night because it was counterproductive. But no amount of sleep aid or meditation or exercise seemed to help him get the full eight hours he needed. Even when he was as exhausted as he felt tonight.

Saying goodbye to Carla and Sidney, they left the boisterous crowd for the quiet comfort of the condo.

# WEDNESDAY, MAY 25<sup>TH</sup>

Alan felt surprisingly refreshed when he woke up at 5:00. He brought his laptop to his bed and copied the notes he'd written down in his notebook the day before. He and Enrique had made some headway on the case, and now he needed to be sure they were on the right track. He still had some questions.

Why was Marko in the building on that Saturday night?

Who or what is Eddie Pearson afraid of?

Did Olson start the fire for David Reagan?

Who's the dealer?

Those key questions needed to be answered to get closer to the truth about the fire and the murder. Alan finally got out of bed and was in the shower minutes later. By 6:30 he was walking into his office with a large cup of Starbuck's coffee and a low-cal roll.

On his desk was the computer report about Marko's phone messages. One number looked familiar, and when Alan scanned his notes, he saw that it was a burner phone that might be traced to Eddie Pearson. Marko had called this number twice on Saturday. Alan would have to talk with Eddie again.

Enrique was the best choice to go to the school and see if Eddie would agree to talk with him without trying to 'lawyer up.' Alan had the feeling once again that Eddie was the connection they needed to move on this case.

When Enrique walked into the office soon after 8:00, he complained about traffic as he tossed his coat onto his desk. "Why do people have to cut in front of me all of the time? We're all going the same direction! If I get there two minutes earlier does that make me the winner or something?" He sat heavily on his chair and then looked over to Alan. "How long have you been here?"

"I got in around 6:30. You know me, I was up early and couldn't stay in bed any longer. But I did get some interesting work done and I think I'm making some connections." Alan told him about meeting Jerome at the theater and reported on his visit to Patricia. On the incident board he had listed the questions they needed to get answered about the case. "I want you to visit Eddie at school again and try to find out if he has a burner phone and if Marko called him Saturday night."

"Do you think Eddie's the key to this mystery? Because we know he's not telling us something and his name keeps popping up repeatedly. Maybe he's just afraid of his father, or maybe he's deep in trouble with a dealer. He's got a bad attitude and that's what gets kids like him into trouble. Does he have any priors?" Enrique was questioning everything now.

"Just some delinquent things his family got him out of. But it's enough to put him on our radar. I wonder who he hangs out with. Maybe the Principal will know. Ask him when you get there."

Olson packed his truck with enough clothes to last for a month. He was smart enough to trade his license plates with another one a dealer had given him. He had been advised to do this often so his truck wouldn't be caught on cameras. Stupid cameras were everywhere now. Even when he checked on the St. Botolph building, he was careful enough to park around the block. If it wasn't cameras that spied on citizens, it was owners of the other buildings. If someone got too suspicious, like that block watch idiot, Olson let him know he managed a building. He was especially careful when he was meeting one of the kids who regularly bought.

Eddie Pearson worried him. If the kid cracked and said he was meeting him at the building the night of the fire, he would be the number one suspect. He called the kid a few times and warned him not to say anything. Pearson was basically weak, and Olson knew he was more afraid of his father than of him. But if he had to, Olson knew ways to go after the whole family. Looking at his watch, he had just enough time to meet the train and get out of the city.

Enrique arrived at the High School just in time for the second period of the day. The Principal met him in the office and led him to a conference room. Concerned

253

about why the police were questioning Eddie again, the Principal wanted to help.

"I don't know Eddie's friends, but I could ask some of the teachers if you think it's important."

"Maybe later," Enrique said, "right now I just need to talk with Eddie."

When Eddie arrived at the conference room, he looked panicked. Enrique stood up and held out his hand. "It's okay, Eddie. Given your reaction at the station, I thought you might prefer to answer some questions here. We can call your dad if you'd like. Please have a seat."

Looking around the room and then watching the Principal close the door, Eddie remained standing. "Do I have to talk to you?" He looked weakly at Enrique and seemed to be exhausted. Finally, he pulled up a chair and sank into it.

"Well, you don't have to, but it would help us to know more about your dealings with Marko. We see there were several calls to a burner phone from Marko's phone on the Saturday he died. Can you tell me if the phone is yours and what the calls were about?" Enrique kept a quiet tone as he looked cautiously at the teen. Finally, Eddie just collapsed his arms and head onto the table in front of him.

"You know, Eddie, there are several good reasons for you to help us out with this case. We know it was arson, and we will find out who set the fire. What we want to know is why Marko was in the building. He knew one of the tenants on the first floor, we've already talked with her. But it was very late at night when the fire was started, and we wonder why Marko would be there at that hour. Do you know why?"

"This is all just a mess!" Eddie blurted out. "I was scared and worried and Marko was just trying to help me. I owed money to this dealer, and he said he would hurt me and my family if I didn't pay him. I was supposed to meet him at the building that night to tell him how I was going to pay what I owed him." Eddie sagged back into his chair and let his hands fall to his sides. "Marko was going to meet me at that building on St. Botolph Street and help me out. He promised there would be no cops. I waited for him to show up, but he never did. And then I saw this guy in the building and he was pouring gasoline all over the floor. I looked in the window and saw Marko's body lying on the floor. The guy went over and poured the stuff on him too. So, I ran."

At this point Eddie was sobbing. Enrique sat back and let Eddie finally relieve himself of the guilt.

"Okay, okay," Enrique quietly said, "Let's find out who this guy was that set the fires. Do you have a pretty good description of him?"

"Yes... he's the one who's after me." Eddie raised his head and wiped his eyes with his shirt sleeve. "I know exactly who he is!"

Eddie named and described Henry Olson. He pulled himself together and accompanied Enrique back to the precinct. He was adamant that he didn't want his father involved and was told he had the right to talk without his father's permission. When Alan met them in an interview room, he looked with confidence at Eddie and told him how much he appreciated his help. Once they had a positive ID on Olson, they would begin sending out bulletins to pick him up.

Olson's truck was picked up in the parking lot outside the Boston Amtrak station. Alan and Enrique scanned video tapes in hopes of finding him. They finally noticed him entering a train for upstate New York. They had been informed that Olson had a brother in Albany. Alerting the Albany police Henry Olson was in the area and was a suspect for a murder and arson investigation, they gave them the address of Olson's brother. Detectives and uniformed officers were sent to the address later that day. When they knocked on the door, they heard someone running through the house.

Olson was captured as he tried to climb out the second story window.

# THURSDAY, MAY 26<sup>TH</sup>

Alan and Enrique spent time reviewing the case. "But now, this almost seems too easy," Enrique was mentally replaying the scene, "what was Olson thinking? Hiding out at his brothers was so obvious."

"You heard he was waiting for a passport and new ID, right? If it wasn't for Eddie coming through, he may have been on his way to who knows where." Alan had a concerned look on his face as he thought of the arrest and the plea bargain Olson was willing to give them. "Whatever scheme they were trying to pull…the fire and forensic reports both confirmed that no trace of extermination agents was found in the building. Olson confirms this. He never called a company to fumigate. So, it was all a cover up for financial gain."

"Olson was smart and immediately pointed the finger at Reagan as the one who came up with the plan. It looks like there'll be insurance and utility fraud on top of arson. David Reagan is going to pay for all the pain he's caused so many people." Alan thought again of Patricia and all her memories that were destroyed in the fire.

"What about that Trudy lady? Is she going to get away with everything?" Enrique was hoping she was involved, even in a small way.

"They just picked her up for possession and distribution of drugs. Olson named her as a contact. But it's unlikely to stick because she's being very clever. She's lawyered up and her building's in the process of being sold to help pay the fees. She'll probably end up just having to pay a fine. I think Marko suspected her as a dealer all along. He found some incriminating information on her from the college she attended. She had quite the business of selling drugs for years, starting at an early age. Money wise, it explains how she could afford the building she owned."

Alan later learned that Trudy had been instructed not to leave the city. Olson had already implicated her as a dealer, and when they searched her place, the police found not only drugs but also lists of contacts that would open many investigations. They were able to identify some of her clients from those lists, and several were offered a plea bargain to testify against her.

Alan stood up and walked to the window. It was another beautiful spring day in Boston. Tourists would be arriving in hordes to visit the historical city and remember why this country was built on such a powerful foundation.

He turned to Enrique, "Solving the case doesn't bring our friend back." This was always the sad reality of police work. Alan looked at the time, he had another appointment with Rose at 5:00.

The first thing Alan said to Rose was in thanks. "I want you to know how much I appreciate the referral you gave me for Sam. He's met with the counselor and started the group therapy. Thank you."

Rose smiled and then focused on Alan. "Tell me, how are you doing?"

"Well, so many events and outcomes in the last few weeks. Finding Marko's killer and the reason for the arson, has kept me pretty busy. Sometimes I find myself staring off into space just thinking about my friend and what a loss his death is to so many people. I miss him."

"It sounds like you found out more about his life than you realized. He appears to have been a wonderful person."

"That's one of the parts of any investigation. As we dig into people's lives, they're often revealed through their actions and the contacts they've made. Sometimes it's for the worse, but in Marko's case, he was quite a hero and a friend to just about everyone."

"What are your plans, now, Alan? You mentioned looking forward to retiring, are you still considering this?"

Alan settled into the comfortable chair and thought. He was working through several possible scenarios, but he was no nearer to enlightenment about his future than before and so he shook his head wearily. "To tell you the truth, I'm just tired. I'm not certain what to do next but I also don't feel like pressuring myself."

Rose understood. "You have a lot to consider. The most compassionate thing you can do now is to rest and try to live as fully and passionately as you are able. The key is to pay attention." Rose smiled at Alan and wondered what his next step would be.

"You have to learn to have patience with yourself, Alan. A relatively new feature of the human experience is that we live longer which sounds both wonderful and terrible." They both laughed at this. "If you learn to pay attention and use your inner strengths, you'll be happier and more productive. How does this sound?"

"I'm going to need your help with this," Alan admitted. "I want to be more adventurous and curious about life. Can you help me do that?"

Rose gave a warm smile. "Let's begin."

# SATURDAY
## (TWO WEEKS LATER)

The Memorial Service for Marko was very well attended. His siblings, along with their children had arrived a week earlier. It looked like a family reunion as they gathered around the outdoor park near Sidney's building. He insisted on a catered reception, inviting the many people who had come into Marko's life. There were several teens from the center and the colorful group from the drag shows. Jerome was dressed in a long flowing silk cape dotted with tiny hearts. Grandma Mae was decked out in a stylish satin pink jacket with a pink rose corsage. She was talking with Patricia Briggs, and they seemed to be getting along like old friends. Alan smiled and was delighted at the thought that they might bond.

Enrique and Marie were also there. Marie was constantly directing her husband to introduce her to people as she inched closer to Jerome and Alicia with interest. They were discussing the new show at the theater that would be highlighting Marko's designs. Alicia had sent invitations to all her clients who were delighted to attend.

Sam and Maryanne also attended the reception. Alan could tell there was a distance between them. Maryanne seemed to be reluctant to engage in conversation and sat in one of the chairs that had been set out. Tony was sitting beside her. Sam wandered around the crowd until he found Carla. She had helped Sidney organize this affair and seemed to be enamored with the handsome lawyer. Alan was amused. He looked around for Lily and finally found her talking animatedly to one of Marko's sisters. Everyone seemed to be offering comfort to each other, and Alan could see the love flowing deeply for Marko. He would have been touched with this event, thought Alan. Marko loved people and now they were honoring him and all he meant to them.

Alan knew he had a lot to be thankful for, too. He waved at Sidney and went to join him.